Silvia Sanza was born in the Bronx and lives in Manhattan. Her previous novel, *Alex Wants to Call It Love*, is also published by Serpent's Tail

TWICE REAL

SILVIA SANZA

Library of Congress Catalog Card Number: 93-84271

A catalogue record for this book can be obtained from the British Library on request.

The right of Silvia Sanza to be identified as the author of this work has been asserted by her in accordance with the Copyright, Designs and Patents Act 1988.

This is a work of fiction. Any resemblance to people living or dead is purely coincidental.

Copyright © 1993 Silvia Sanza

First published 1993 by Serpent's Tail,
4 Blackstock Mews, London N4, and
401 West Broadway #1, New York, NY 10012

Imageset in 11/14pt Bembo by Image Setters Ltd, London EC1
Printed in the United States of America

FOR JOHN

CHAPTER 1

At the time of "Blue," I was very west, which is emotion, and as a result I couldn't communicate with the northeast, which is more rational and business oriented.

*Joni Mitchell,
tracing her artistic growth*

"You can yell till you're blue in the face," his mother used to tell Willy Saunders.

So he used to yell until he was blue in the face.

That's just what he wanted to do now. He was in jail for Christmas and he was thinking about that girl and how she had fucked him up. He was still furious.

He remembered how they had met — she was standing half off the curb and he was trying to talk her into crossing the street while the light changed. She had looked at him like he was crazy but she did it, following him across Fourteenth Street. They started talking at the next light. Not too long after, he decided he would let her in on his idea. He needed her help. They would go into Bloomingdale's together and when the coast was clear, stuff whatever they could of the expensive stuff into a big shopping bag. She would carry it; he would pick up something small and hide it under his jacket. They would walk very near each other, almost side by side, together out of the store and set the alarm off; she would sail out, leaving the security guard to assume the alarm went off for him. He would admit to being guilty and get caught with something petty, and she would walk away with thousands. The plan had started working better and better; he envisioned them as Bonnie and Clyde, smooth, graceful and debonair. And she was slick — she even had a friend Doris who told her right down to brand names what to steal. It was a sure thing. They would clean up. Hit the jackpot. And he thought it up all by himself. That was half a year ago. But the girl got scared. Or maybe it was something else. Maybe it was more deliberate, maybe even premeditated. That was the kind of deliberateness he would never forgive. Maybe she was just out to get him. She had left him there, holding the bag. Literally.

He was thinking hard about Marabea. He would sit down and write her a letter she couldn't resist. He wanted to be sure she didn't forget him.

CHAPTER 2

Success is Knowing Which Appointments to Keep

An ad for Quorum, a perfume,
"the essence of success"

Marabea was on the way to the basement of the Catholic church where the Saturday morning meetings of her diet club were held. She opened her mailbox. There was a small white box from Figi's, the mail order food catalogue in Marshfield, Wisconsin. It said "Congratulations, your first round winner prize is enclosed." Then she saw the word "perishable" so she knew it was food. She hoped it would be cheese or something nutritious because whatever it was she knew she would eat it right away. It turned out to be Fudgie Rabbit, one and a half ounces of soft moist fudge. There were two rabbits and she ate them both. She tried to figure out how many calories each rabbit was. She should probably talk about it at the meeting. She should probably also tell the truth about eating a pound and a half of grapes yesterday. She hadn't wanted that many but the fruit vendor took a big bunch which weighed out to a pound and a half. She didn't know how to say that was more than she wanted even though she knew she would eat the whole thing. But better grapes than mallomars which was really the mood she was in.

At this morning's meeting three girls sobbed in quick succession. One of the three rested her head in the nook of the shoulder of the woman next to her and kept it there for the remaining hour. Another one said she had seen a TV show about a man eating a snake and that's how food felt to her; repulsive as the idea of eating was, she was worried that she didn't have enough money for food.

Marabea had been going to the meetings for a couple of months and by now had become easily bored listening to people talk; she was indifferent to everyone. She didn't care what anybody was suffering through nor did she really want to talk about herself. She knew only that she must get thin; if she was thin, she would be like everybody else. The problem was she could never stay in control for as long as it took. Her father had owned a candy store in Brooklyn and she was sure that was why she loved sweets the way she did. Being thin was hauntingly inaccessible.

When she had first arrived in the city, she had answered an "Apartment Share" ad in one of the downtown newspapers. Her future roommate asked only that the rent be on time, that she didn't smoke and that she have no pets. She ignored Marabea after that. The ad had said "access to roof" and that intrigued Marabea. She loved the image of a bawdy sophisticated New York rooftop. It was glamour to her. She loved glamour; she was obsessed by old Hollywood movies, the flourish of devotion gone astray midst healthy unembellished vice. She knew things like one of Danny Thomas's early jobs in radio was making the sound of horses' hooves on the *Lone Ranger* show by beating his chest with two toilet plungers.

She tried to make a living at cleaning apartments but she knew she wasn't very good at it. She had to keep advertising for new clients: sticking her name, telephone number and made-up qualifications on mailboxes, in the supermarket, and on telephone poles. She decorated her ads with crayons and made them attractive in a childish way. She wanted everyone to think they were getting an artist to do their housecleaning. She added in pink magic marker "Attention to detail." Once in a while if she needed extra work, she would go to an employment agency — she thought it would be nice to clean offices in big Park Avenue buildings late at night when most of the city was sleeping — but they seemed to want only Polish ladies. All the cleansers and disinfectants ruined her fingernails. She often found herself staring into space with her fingers in her mouth. Her dentist warned her she was putting so much force on her teeth when she bit her fingernails she was prying her teeth loose. But she couldn't stop. As soon as they started to grow, she bit them before they were even nails. Sometimes when she got very anxious she would go up on the roof. She could see the tops of trees and hear street sounds coming up instead of across. She saw angles in misty distance. She was fascinated with the way the sky was cut up when she was eye to eye with it.

When she was much younger, everyone told her she had a great sense of humor, but that was gone now. She had never had a best friend. She longed for entitlements.

When she came home that night, there was a letter in her mailbox. It was folded in half, the four corners turned down, folded again and stapled. She pried open the staples and began reading it; it was printed in pencil on cheap ruled looseleaf paper.

>Dear Marabea,
>I do feel pretty down when you're not here with me. I hope you're feeling the same when im away. I think that love puts us in that moode, Do you think so? Theres a book with our name in it, It's the book of love. When im alone i sing my sadest song for you and i because your not there for me. Its funny how I miss you so much it seems the more i tell you the more you'll remember. time is like the wind and we must sav it ok, The more that we save the more that we'll have Do you think so. Only GOD coud tell you how much i care for you, and if there were away for him to tell you buy talking to you i believe that he would. Like the wind you're always on my mind, and never should i ever forget you. From now until Hell frezzes over i'll always protect you., So let the fog no longer blind you and let me guid you on all the way, Lord knows if I had one wish it would be to hold you in my arms for life to stay.
>>I Love You
>>>Alway Marabea
>>>>And let no day
>>>>>Go buy with out
>>>>>>Me your Love
>>>>>>>Telling you
>>>>>>>>So.
>>>>>>>>>Willy

She lay the letter down on a table and curled up on the sofa and began watching *The Goldwyn Follies* (1938). Zorina would be the highlight, the television guide said, "in a superb water nymph ballet by Balanchine." A young boy with freckles and complicated eyes with too much white came on the TV saying he used to sit in his room for two days in a row smoking crack and how he is now recovered and how happy he is to be recovered. Marabea wondered if she had anything in her life she should be recovering from. She wanted to stop eating and she wanted to stop stealing. She couldn't believe that she had really gone into Kentucky Fried Chicken and stolen one thousand seven hundred dollars and forty cents from the cashier. She didn't have any money and needed some just to get by; the rest of it she just wanted to blow away. Another time she had held up a gas station and gotten six hundred dollars. That was the morning she woke up and felt she had never looked uglier and thought if she got some money it would make her feel better — money with its deadly accurate fragile glory. Another time she pushed in a front door of an apartment in her mother's building and took a camera and some pretty good jewelry. Then one day she walked into a police net and was charged with attempting to rob a discount jewelry store, and that had scared her but only for a while. Now she could feel the old unblinking poke — she wanted to do something bad. It didn't have to be stealing. It just had to satisfy that relentless anxiety that was compelling her, an elemental impulse with a mind of its own.

The movie began, music and lyrics by the Gershwins, and the first shot was a spacious lobby. Spacious lobbies excited her.

At her next diet club meeting, some woman Theresa talked on and on like a tired motor. Marabea often saw her at meetings and thought she talked too much. All she did was complain about her brother Martin going out with a girl too young for him or her son Andy and his humorless girlfriend. While she listened to Theresa's tedious narrative about how her husband never used soap when he washed a dish, she felt angry. She felt like having an outburst. She started thinking about making a bomb. She wanted to do damage; it didn't much matter to whom. Theresa's voice was adrift. All these people were after stolen dreams. That made them arrogant. Conventional. Exasperating. It would really be great if she could make a bomb. Just to see if she could do it.

CHAPTER THREE

"Take Cover.
This Is No Ordinary Day In the Sun."

Ad for the film
Savage Beach

Andy and his friends were talking about when was a condom too old for safe sex. You carried it around and carried it around and carried it around.

They have a shelf life of about five years, one of the guys said. Was shelf life the same kind of life as carrying it around in a wallet? Was it all right to squeeze it to death? Someone volunteered that in Uganda they called condoms "socks." He had a girlfriend who was fifteen years old and a rock groupie; he was proud of her because she got into the hospitality room of his favorite group by sleeping with a roadie on the tour bus. The roadie had told her she was a smokin' gun. He repeated the story with an exuberant smile.

Andy and his friends lived in a very nice section of New Jersey where there were vines on the houses and nothing was skimpy. Life was roses in bloom and never a dead zone. They were all part of some modern relationship. New Jersey Transit stopped at their door. They grew up with the dynamics of mobility, lyrical subversives seduced by pushing the limits. The minute they were old enough, they all had cars and when they weren't talking about sex and rock 'n' roll, they were thinking about the future, a time warp of powerful days with the fun of disorder that would never betray them.

Andy no longer was concerned about what his mother felt about anything he got caught up in; but he was aware of the structure of her density; she was the edge of his thoughts. He had finally reached an age — how long he stayed there remained to be seen — where his feelings were experiments with power. He felt neither defensive nor benign and was alarmed at the feelings that kept coming up, tired metaphors with ambitious inroads. He didn't know how to tell anyone about them.

Andy had just broken up with a girl who had been in analysis twice a week. She wore round glasses and cashmere sweaters. Her name was Krista. Her family had plenty of money; both her parents were investment analysts. She was going to Barnard. Whatever her friends did, all of them terminally collegiate eighteen and nineteen year olds, she did. If they went swimming after school, she went swimming after school. There was global laughter. They liked to go out to eat things with faintly exotic names — exotic to her, intrusive to him — like Sicilian smoked fish, orange flavored rye bread and glazed banana tarts. He had originally been attracted to her because she seemed to read a lot — really read; there were bookmarks in her books and they were always hardcover. Even though they were the same age she was the more sophisticated, and although at first the poise attracted him, he soon wearied of the peculiar charm of her energy. He was only eighteen and wanted very much to confide in her, to tell her how he always felt like he was walking into the wind and how sometimes he could barely deal with the mad pounding in his chest. The day they broke up she had been cooing at her best friend, happy transparencies ablaze in a haze of mutual adoration, telling each other how wonderful they looked and tugging or petting each other's hair in the bargain. It made him sick. He listened to them talk about Septembers that were years away. Her friend was thinking pre-med but was worried because it had taken her a year to read *Anna Karenina*. Andy didn't feel as smart as any of them; he absorbed a great deal of life but he had almost flunked algebra and had no interest in a Ph.D. He wished he could find someone to worship, a girl who didn't mind reading used paperbacks, wasn't afraid of illicit-looking people and didn't mind being alone once in a while, a girl he wouldn't outgrow. He was angry at everything that went on between his ex-girlfriend and her ever present gang of hypersensitive girlfriends who excelled in a shared state-of-the-art heritage.

He was angry at his mother, too. Theresa was always involved with her "meetings", which gave her something to say about everyone; everyone, she was discovering, immediate and otherwise, was tarnished with something. Her great aunt was schizophrenic and a brother-in-law from her first marriage annoyed her with his smugness — he went to aerobics three times a week; "the knees were designed to hold no more than ninety pounds," he would tell you. She felt her time would be used wisely attending 12-step meetings as a co-dependent and learning about the perilous addictions she was appalled to find really existed. She had a spiritual leader and prayed to St. Jude and St. Augustine.

Her best friend's husband was a drinker who divorced her after twenty-eight years and this best friend, too shy to go alone, took Theresa to her first Al Anon meeting. After that engrossing introduction, she became triumphant with moral purity and found everyone she knew in the middle of some lamentable disengagement. Her brother Martin Worthy had lost his eleven year old daughter Elsa in a freak explosion. She still shook when she thought of it. The little girl had spent many weekends with her Aunt Theresa in New Jersey and she had enjoyed having the child around; she loved little girls, singular shining memories of what she had been. She could see Elsa's big prankish eyes and hear her jokes. Did you hear the joke about the playing cards? Never mind, it was no big deal. And they both would giggle. What did the duck say to the clerk after he bought some Chap Stick? Put it on my bill. Theresa always liked little girls better than little boys, which was sad because she had a little boy of her own.

Theresa was after completeness. When would it happen, rugged and grand? Straight out of show business? There always seemed to be something missing; the sunniest days puzzled her. Nothing was ever quite topped off. She went to church every Sunday and listened closely to the wisdom imparted from the pulpit. She wanted to be happier but she questioned if more happiness was what God wanted of her. She liked to pray "thy will be done." She wanted to do somebody's will. One Sunday her favorite priest had said "Take up the burdens of others and yours will be lighter." Another time: "Remember that God is good and He never punishes us as we punish others." This sermon tranquilized her even as she understood that she wanted to be good only because she would be punished if she was otherwise. Yet she was frustrated because she was not allowed to be bad. She was always fanning impulses. She fretted that bad people just might end up getting away with it. This possibility made her sneer and she would not accept it as reasonable. Clarity demanded punishment; punishment was logical. To think otherwise would have been to realign gospel. She knew for sure there was a God; what she needed was the certainty that God would mete out punishment as she saw fit. She wanted sinners unmasked. She had always had a problem seeing people getting away with things, as far back as grade school wanting to please the nuns, spending extra time on those long three-part essay questions and then being coaxed into letting someone copy her homework. Her religious feelings were a staggering system of pulleys in motion. She hated sin of all kinds and loathed it in herself as well as in others. She did not accept it as unavoidable human failing. She would imagine scaling heights not meant to be achieved and examine her conscience and exhaust its horizons as she had been taught as a child. Every morning after chapel the nuns would tell the children to put their heads on the desk and think about their sins. She was never sure how long this ritual should take and she never wanted to be the first to lift her head and open her eyes. She kept her cheek against the shiny wooden desk and clung to unnamed prayer. It was unacceptable to find you had no sins. Everyone had sins, some profound impurity or measured shortcoming that would sneak its way into your heart. She reflected on the mechanics of sin, its derivation. Sin could imitate others — you saw it and were tempted to want to do it — or it could come clear out of your own dismayed heart; it was divine comedy struggling for air. Sin could be hurried and unhurried and her rational attempts to stay away from it held her spellbound. On Sundays the priest would urge "Think of the words of the Lord's Prayer and use them. Read the scriptures. You will find the answers if you open the pages." She prayed a lot for her son Andy who once came right out and told her he was depressed. "I can't see what someone your age has to be depressed about," she told him. "I know you can't understand it," he said, "but Uncle Martin would." Once she had heard Martin telling Andy that life was what went on in your head. For some reason he wanted to yank the boy back from reality. She wondered if it was her fault that Andy didn't feel closer to her. But she was fearful of his intimacies and did not encourage them; she was afraid he would ask her a question she did not know the answer to.

In her kitchen she listened to the radio: "A body of a young man who was handcuffed was found on the roof of a building in Queens." Right away she thought it might be Andy. Any time she heard anything bad, she thought it was happening to Andy. She worried about him constantly, although they inhabited different domains, each absorbed in his own breezy irreverent world. She wished Andy felt closer to his stepfather, Theresa's second husband, Spence. But it was Martin to whom Andy was drawn. Martin was honest about the unsettled state of his own thinking, and made laughingly clear his doubts about balance being a desired state after all. He confused his sister but never Andy, who only wanted more.

The telephone rang; it was Martin. "The meatloaf didn't turn out as good as when you make it," he said.

"How many eggs did you put in?"

"None."

"Mmm, well, how did you hold the breadcrumbs together?"

"I didn't put any breadcrumbs. I put two slices of Arnold's white bread." She was upset at her brother Martin, angry that he was going out with a redhead (she had seen pictures) fifteen years, at least, younger than he was.

Through the window she watched Spence outside surveying his lawn. He couldn't wait for spring when he would give it the first cut. He always started with the mower down to three inches. The lawn looked its worst after the first cut and its best after the final cut at summer's end. She pulled at the crotch of her leotards; it was tight and she was uncomfortable.

Last night they had had a conversation. Theresa started it. He had helped her carry the dinner dishes to the sink which he didn't always do and they had sat down at the dinner table to have their coffee.

"Where would you like to live when we retire?"

"I don't like Florida but I've never been to the west coast."

"The west coast is more humid."

"They're talking a lot about Miami these days. Last week CBS morning news had their whole show from down there."

"Miami . . . with all those Cubans. . ."

"Well, what do you want to do?"

"Maybe learn to play the piano." Theresa paused and ended it with, "I'd like to travel, you know, call AAA and have them map out a trip."

She thought about last Sunday's sermon. It was about forgiveness. Somebody, she supposed it was Peter, asked the Lord, "Lord, I have forgiven him seven times — isn't that enough?" And the Lord said, "70 times 7 isn't enough." Or, something to that effect. She liked that answer; she enjoyed subservience, turning the other cheek. She was sustained by being overturned. Maybe when Spence was finished looking at the lawn, they could go for ice cream. It was winter but she was always interested in ice cream.

The next afternoon Theresa was sitting in the living room worrying about her hair. It was getting grayer and grayer and even when she had the energy to color it, it looked like a whisk broom. She would be fifty years old soon and she was fifteen pounds overweight, some days twenty. She liked the way she smelled and she still polished her toenails. She often contemplated her youth, longing for what had gone before, engulfed in rousing memory of an old boyfriend whose name was hazy but whose image was sharp. She remembered how earnest his eyes when he wanted to make love; she could feel him in her, as though he were there, right now, between her legs in stone. She wanted abundance, brilliant and sympathetic. The past had been unfair by going so fast.

She tried to concentrate on her favorite weekday afternoon

talk show but the garbage trucks were drowning it out. Today's guest was a transsexual who was not being allowed to visit her boyfriend in prison for something called aggravated robbery. A Waldbaum's ad flashed across the screen. Come share our values. Next she watched a game show. The puzzle was "Their job is to make waves." The answer was curlers.

She let herself be distracted. Someone on television said "From my perspective I have no long term point of view." She thought of the few love letters she had gotten from boys she had known and how whatever they wrote sounded earth-shakingly right. She wondered if Andy understood how important it is to send, to receive and to keep birthday and Christmas cards. They were the proof of time, the time that illuminated us; it was vivid in its disappearance. It was disarming — there had never been less of it. The critical thing was that she had lost the ability to compete; now it was layered defense. An ad on TV: the thing about roads is they often come with bumps.

She wished she could lose her appetite, but all she thought about lately was food. She could feel how much weight she was gaining. Her slips were tight and her breasts and belly were one. With Spence a barbed relaxation had wiped out what dreams there had been of superior passion. So she drank coffee and paced. The coffee was instant and she drank it from a delicately shaped china cup with pink and white dogwood climbing up a blue stem. She wished she could feel Spence's fingers scrambling inside her panties where they hadn't been for a long time. She managed a sip of coffee and then, again, she wanted to pace. She read the *Sunday Times*, which was still laying around even though it was Wednesday, a quarter of a page at a time. Her eyes dotted four spots on each page, top left, top right, bottom left, bottom right. Priscilla Presley was introducing "a fragrance as versatile as Priscilla herself." It was called Moments. Theresa paced some more. Her leotards were tight even standing up. Her underwear was tight. She had thrown two old pairs of panties away just that weekend. She had looked at them and realized they were so stretched out they were nothing more than rags. A yellow rag with a white band and a blue rag with a lighter blue band. She got up and went into the closet and took out her Persian lamb coat, the one with the white fox collar, and went into her bedroom and looked in the mirror. She bundled the fur around her face and smiled. One of the things she liked about winter was that she got to wear her Persian lamb coat. She liked the way she looked in it, as though any minute now a handsome man would link his arm in hers and take her for a drink. When winter was over, this small indulgence would go with it.

She watched the winter weather change the view from her window. A minute ago there had been sunlight. The tips of the goldenrod shone; the stones were spotted with light; the grass shimmered and shadows were strong. Then a gray sheet came over the sky and everything shut down. She supposed her jumpiness was menopause. She never said the word except to herself and then only in her head. It was just one of those facts of life, neither good nor bad, something like an eclipse, really.

CHAPTER 4

The physicists shined a light and looked for the electrons and they said "Wait a minute! We're not getting any signal."

*From a story called "Giant Moments"
in the Physics Watch column of Discover magazine*

New Year's Eve at Wetlands. Martin felt like everybody's grandfather. His toes kept getting stepped on in the dark while he tried to act gracious and not notice. He marveled at how graceful everybody was, exploding bodies snaking in and out of impossible crowds with handsome youthful grace. He wondered how long Fiarette would want to stay; she seemed so at ease bopping up and down on the frontlines close to the music. One boy was trying to flirt with her and she gave him only a polite smile. Martin wondered what she would be doing if he wasn't there. Early in the evening at her apartment, they had made egg nog, starting with a quart of store-bought to which she had added a pint of heavy cream which she whipped in her blender. The recipe said to add eight ounces of dark rum but she had no rum so she put in twelve ounces of French brandy. Martin was a beer drinker but the egg nog had been terrific and he wished he had some now. The music was loud and people smelled of tacos and salty snacks and everyone was right on top of him. From where he stood, Martin could watch Fiarette take a taco and scoop it with something from the buffet. She brought the food to her mouth with her right hand and then pushed it along her tongue with her index finger.

Fiarette was trying to have fun but she was sorry she had suggested they come; it was as though they weren't even together, and yet she could not deny his presence: he was standing right there. She should have paid attention when he said he wanted something quieter — a celebration at a church on East 16th Street — but she wanted to dance. How could you not spend at least some part of New Year's Eve dancing and flinging yourself at mirrors? It was tradition. But these days there was no room to dance any more — at least she never found any — no more unlimited reckless space where it was a kick to get struck by lightning, where you could choose your subject and be a poet. She remembered her best friend Kary and all their New Year's Eves together. Neither one of them ever had a serious enough boyfriend on New Year's Eve and they always seemed to end up with each other. Kary was gone, dead, murdered. Fiarette was still angry at Kary for leaving her, as though the murdered girl had purposefully chronicled the final rip in her life and cashed in on some rude privilege. She remembered the time Kary came up to her office on her birthday and surprised her with a bouquet of daisies and a copy of *In Watermelon Sugar*. She could not get Kary out of her thoughts. She could not bear the thought that anyone's life could be over so swiftly, without warning, without definition, without rules, making a small world swallow hard.

ten days later

The best and worst of the holidays was over and the world was falling apart. A war was brewing. Navy ships were decorated for the holidays, no one was being enlightened, there was no sense to chronology and there were faked embraces. It was hard to be happy even when you had no reason not to be. Even the weather was crazy — fifty six degrees one day, thirty the next.

Martin Worthy was looking at his girlfriend of just about a year; she got under his skin like jazz; his thoughts got harder and he wondered why she couldn't manage to love him.

Fiarette hadn't meant to go to sleep with her back toward him but lately she seemed to get tired first and she liked to sleep on her left side. Martin would get in and would sleep on his left side, too, loop his arm around her, never too tight. He would pat her ass a couple of times, then rub it, and if she responded he would do more. Minutes later he would be snoring and when the snoring was finished, his breathing would be like a child's and he would be very still and his face, surrendered of the puzzles of being awake, drained and delivered of age, would look like the young man he had once been. She enjoyed his maleness and its celebrated vulnerability. She loved to touch him when he was asleep. She would rub his stomach. The hair on his stomach felt good under her palms and in his sleep he would moan approval. He never seemed to wake up during the night but she often did. Last night she had woken up and stepped out of bed, folding closed the wooden shuttered doors behind her. In the other room she sat on the loveseat, a pin dot navy, and found herself wondering how long he had had it; the arm rests were threadbare and in some spots there was no blue left. She wished he would get a new one. She sat down and picked up the magazine article she had been reading about Farrah Fawcett and Ryan O'Neal. Farrah was saying it was stupid they never got married. "The closest we came was Reno. But we ran out of gas." Fiarette climbed back to bed thinking how lucky Farrah was to look so sexy in those pictures on the beach.

That was last night. This New York Sunday morning Fiarette was still asleep, curled, one knee bare and the other barely covered by the burgundy robe she had fallen asleep in. For Martin, just her sleeping presence gave the room fragrance. He wondered if her love was the only way she knew how, passion one night and temper the next. He worried that he was boring her, that to need her was to fail her. He wondered if she was absorbing his love, feeling less lonely because of it. He wondered who needed whom more. He wanted to see through her contemporary eyes because he did not know who it was up to. He wanted contentment to mean more than resignation, more than allegiance and the everlasting loop of scrutiny. It must mean positive and even amusing resolutions.

Martin's apartment looked much the same as it had when his wife and daughter were alive. The same afghan was still on the bed, the yellow, pink and orange squares with wide black stripes that his wife's aunt in Chatham had given them as a wedding present. He still had Elsa's teddy bear on his bureau with the red satin bow she had pinned to his chest — and a papier maché Easter egg he had given his wife, with a picture of a little girl who looked like Shirley Temple smelling flowers on it. The furniture was the same, the bedroom, the little living room with the old navy pin dot a little bigger than a loveseat, the dining room. Every bit of it was there: things discovered through ads in the *Voice* or found on the street or bought at thrift shops — he had not gotten rid of a thing. Martin would never move out of this apartment. In his study were plastic crates full of notes on yellow lined paper, magazines folded back to stories he did not want to forget, a Minnesota Twins World Series 1987 mug he kept pencils in and his bright blue Pilot Spotlighter. He was always highlighting something somewhere. There were as many books on the floor as in the bookcase. mostly paperbacks he would pick up from booksellers on the street. Yesterday he bought *The Painted Bird* by Jerzy Kosinski. He didn't always read everything all the way through. The story didn't matter to him. Most of the time he would pick up a book in the middle just to hear the sound of someone else's thoughts on paper.

Elsa's room would always be Elsa's room, but now the desk

he had built for her out of planks of wood was where he typed his stories. He was glad the desk fit him, too. He liked sitting there in the space that had been hers. Elsa was dead; it had helped teach him submissiveness. Being tractable was something Fiarette had yet to learn. She was always after him to change the linoleum in the kitchen. "It's curling up at the edges. Let's go look at tile," she would urge. When she got seriously upset she would say, "Why do you like to live like a slob?" And he thought about it but decided he didn't like changing things. When surroundings and environment remained the same, time seemed to pass more slowly. He liked that. And so for reasons like that he would always save the little three-drawer cabinet that his wife had never been able to find the right spot for. She stuck it in front of a window. It was still there and that was where he wanted it left; he couldn't guess what was in its drawers. But it reminded him of the way things had been, how days merely overlapped and didn't really go too far after all. Good and bad, witty hearts and swelling ordeals, things had happened and they were a grid he needed; he was afraid of smudging their memory by something so insignificant as placing a stick of furniture against a different wall. And the cane chair that was broken — he just stuck a big pillow with fringe on the seat and someone always managed to sit on the chair and sag right into the broken cane. Fiarette kept telling him to throw it out or get it repaired; he liked it the way it was. He wanted her to understand that filling in the reticent gaps in a new lifestyle is what changes you, not a furious attempt at new furniture.

"Sometimes I wonder why you don't like yourself more," she told him, "you never like to do anything nice for yourself." She ground the word "nice" out with her teeth.

"But I'd do anything for you."

And that was true. He'd hand her tens and twenties and if she stopped to admire something in a store window it was always, "Let's go in and get it for you." And always with a smile.

"But that isn't the point. I want you to do things for yourself."

"But my kitchen floor doesn't matter to me."

"But I want it to matter."

Fiarette knew that there'd never be a day in her life when she'd hear the song Funky Sensation and wouldn't want to dance.

They had started last night at her apartment, but had ended it at his. In their year together there had never been an easy flow to things like where they would spend their time together, whose apartment they would go to and how long they would stay there, where they would sleep, and if they would sleep together. Much of the time there was serious ambiguity with half-hearted asides. Spending all night together wasn't, had never been, not even in the early days, an intimacy he allowed himself to assume. And however abruptly an evening ended or however short a weekend was cut, Fiarette always acted as though it was quite obvious that their time together would end precisely when it did. How could he not have seen it? She seemed able to unravel the hazards and calculate the speed of sound, while Martin often felt as though he was missing the more than adequate clues.

Fiarette kept a couple of pair of shoes in Martin's bedroom; her hi top black Reeboks and her white Nikes. The hi tops were her dress shoes. She had one drawer, the top right, in Martin's dresser; he had wanted to give her more room but she said she didn't need more. She hung two things on the hook behind his bedroom door: a pin-striped cotton flannel nightshirt and a Fifties peach silk robe from Antique Boutique that an old boyfriend had given her. Having something there that another man had given her allowed her to feel detached;

she wanted a tantalizing involvement but she wanted the sanctuary of remoteness. She wanted to be devoted and true, but ruthless and exhausting to decode. She kept some of her jars and bottles on the windowsill behind his tub, things she couldn't do without, her jasmine body oil and the morello cherry lip balm from The Body Shop. But some things that she had thought she couldn't do without she did very well without when they ran out. Like the lavender soap. So much had been urgent in the crucial first months of their affair; she would never go to sleep without jasmine oil at every pulse point until one day she woke up thinking it was a frail prop whose time was about up.

But Martin, although he was willing to concede that the two of them didn't always look that happy in photographs any more, was not ready to let go. Instead, he felt tension and longing and neither was pleasurable. Whatever would be with Fiarette would be but he believed he had the power to delay it. His temperament, he felt, would never make him capable of easy transition, lingering one day with happiness and the next with controlled opposition. It was post-holiday season, a time when people felt compelled to change direction and search for "opportunities to succeed." The grim determination to stick with it just because it was the holidays was already two weeks old. It was time for the live details.

He had had enough of the newspaper, a story in the *New York Times* Magazine about Halston and another in the business section about the bankrupt Hilton Head Island. He read the Book Review and the promise of a new Stephen King novel, "Once you lock your door . . . the real terror begins." He was turning pages and seeing nothing. He had to be in a certain mood to read about Senate races starting early and lenders illegally collecting billions in excess escrow payments on home loans. Lonely, he lay down next to her on the bed hoping to wake her up, but Fiarette did not stir. He thought maybe they would walk over to First Avenue and have cheese blintzes for breakfast. He heard the words of "God Bless America" going off in his head and thought of carefully orchestrated but slightly tilted campaigns.

Fiarette always went to bed first and got up last when they slept at his apartment and she always went to bed last and got up first when they were at hers. He loved when she woke up happy because when she was happy she would put make-up on. Martin loved to watch this. She would put cream all over her face, wipe it off, and, with a long-handled oval brush, brush on loose powder that looked like it had strands of gold in it. She would dab perfume oil on each wrist and then inside each wrist. And as the scent lingered and she realized how much she liked it, she would dab more behind her ears and on the points of each shoulder. Martin enjoyed the sensuality of a woman making herself beautiful. She knew he was there, but she never seemed to grasp how closely she was being watched. But Martin knew the odds were that she would wake up angry, although her anger — meditative and literate — could calm him down. Sometimes she would just announce, "I'm in a bad mood." She insisted this kind of honest announcement was a good thing to do because it absolved the other person of blame; it meant she was enlightened; she was, by saying these words, accepting full responsibility for what was making her snarl.

In bed, awake but not wanting Martin to know it, Fiarette was feeling bleak. She was thinking of her fortune from the cookie last night when she and Martin took home Chinese food: "Friends long absent are coming back to you." She was wondering whether she was more afraid of life or of death when she fell asleep again.

Later Fiarette woke up realizing she no longer felt sexy

around Martin. The actions were too familiar. She did not feel wronged — it did not feel like a tragic secret — but she was after a moonlight walk. First she thought it was her and then she thought it was him and then she realized it was them; he was no longer a significant pursuit. He didn't seem to need sex and neither, she was forced to admit, did she. Sex demanded a fundamental energy and she was too tired to play, too tired to be spirited, not interested in being capricious and breaking down the gates of some hollow paradise. She knew Martin would welcome her advances but she knew him so well now that while there was still room for surprise, the surprise fell flat, like when the bubbles were done with the champagne. She had lost a great deal in the year before she started going out with Martin Worthy and suffered while she probed at how existence ends up a pile of circumstances. She had lost friends, people who were her reflection, and she wondered how joy could come when sanity had been interrupted.

Martin watched Fiarette read the Travel section. It was the only part of the paper that really held her interest. She read Q and A about people who wanted to get tickets to the Grand Prix or people who were bumped from connecting flights and wanted to know what they could do about it. She read the travel advisory and the weather watch and the value of a dollar around the world. Martin knew she loved to travel and he was in the mood himself; maybe he should take her away and not let the war news stop him. More than twenty countries were on the State Department's list of nations to be avoided as a result of the Gulf conflict.

"How much time do you think it's okay to spend thinking about the past?" Fiarette asked Martin, pouring her second mug of coffee and putting the Travel section down.

"How much time do you spend thinking about the past?"

"I'm sure it's more than most people. Maybe too much. How do I know. . . " She shook her long red hair away from her face.

"I can't comment on that. Some people need to embrace the past continually; some people soon as they think of it they're done with it. And some people never think about it at all, Maybe it scares them — maybe it never occurs to them. And maybe they know they'll never figure it out."

"What about you . . . do you think about the past a lot?"

"Sometimes." It was a myth, he wanted to tell her, the past was nothing more than a myth — a myth and a blur.

"Like when?"

"When something triggers it."

"Well, that's me, too, only so many things seem to trigger it. Like Alex. Alex killed himself." She repeated blindly, "He killed himself. He jumped off a roof and covered the pavement." She looked at but not out the window. Alex who could turn words into song, dead, at last isolated from madness; the second anniversary of his death would be July fourth. His death had burned a predominant space in her head. Her eyes narrowed. "I was so fragmented that summer. I'm not sure I felt it at all when it happened. It's almost more of a shock now than it was then. I thought he was just another crazy person who came into my life, but he was different; he was one of a kind, more special than I gave him credit for and that's what hurts so much. I can't believe the deliberateness of what he did."

And then without warning she announced "I guess I'll be going home," and stood up. "But it's only eleven o'clock in the morning." "Oh, I have stuff to do." And, as always, Martin figured he should have seen this coming.

She had to be alone; she could feel the command of clutter, an artificial intelligence so shrewd it was forcing her to think only about the things that hurt. Alone, she began to think about Alex, who as a child fantasized about Superman coming to rescue him and had always wanted to work for DC Comix. Alex, making a series of wrong turns, honest and dark; and how, ill-equipped though he was, with his rough and tumble confidence was able to make street life a charmed and natural landscape. She remembered how he had told her about the dangers of styrofoam, how styrene got into your pores every time you drank from a paper cup. They played lotto with high hopes and Alex always made sure they signed the back of the lotto ticket; that way, if it was lost and they did win, no one else could cash it in.

She remembered Alex the incurable romantic: how one night they made love by the window where the moon murmured high. The bamboo blinds were rolled up and the moonlight was the only light in the room; how well Alex understood the light. She remembered not love, but sensuality. Sweeter than lust, fit for a king, the way sex was meant to be, the kind of sex where the stuff you do makes you feel passionate and irresistible.

She remembered the year before meeting Martin as horror masquerading as life.

And then came Martin and with Martin life was happy. Middle class happy, an earnest and ideal setting, sustaining and safe. But, while she wanted to feel safe, she did not want to surrender to safe. Safety was too middle class, an academic life with pale faced supporters who guaranteed nothing. Safe was not what she wanted. It carried the reputation of being without hope. It forced you to operate out of a restricted area where you loved at arm's length, a well behaved fan. No harm could ever come to you; you would have plenty of advance warning and you could always jump out of the way.

It wasn't so much the sex she wanted as the monumental moments leading up to it. An extended series of discoveries. Instead she was jumpy, at times frantic; conclusions were illusions. Nothing seemed suitable over any length of time. It was a position worse than indecision. It was miscellaneous comfort and she did not know what to do.

Later that day, ten days into a new year, Fiarette was stoned on some grass a friend had brought back from Portland. She took a deep toke and mused about a generation of people who had never gotten high. They were visible to her now as people unwilling to reveal themselves. All those nineteen sixties right wingers, warned that it was morally unsuitable to have a spontaneous reaction. Maybe Martin was one of them.

She floated out the door and headed for Sixth Avenue. On the way she overheard someone say "Work is for people who don't ski."

In Bagel Buffet Fiarette got a sesame bagel. It was still warm. She sat at the front window in a booth that seated four and was almost always taken. She looked out at the corner of Sixth Avenue where Christopher Street and Greenwich Avenues meet. Someone had written "Sid" on a telephone pole. She saw more old ladies and cars than anything else. She knew she could never leave New York. An ambulance siren went off. A guy in a brown leather jacket walked by with his fingers in his ears. A cop leaned against a lamp post that said "Clear fire lane for emergency vehicles." Sunday afternoon was for the tourists; it didn't take long before three girls sat at her table. One of them is Sandy; one of them is Linda. No one ever called the third one by name. They are talking about shipments at Donna Karan. Three white organza shirts, one of which was featured in a video, a "must" shirt one of them called it. Then they discussed Kamali: "I'm not too excited with her line this year, not the jackets, they're so fuzzy." "But that wool crêpe suit," Sandy said. And Linda: "It needs to be exciting; it needs a little zip."

Fiarette got up to get another coffee and took her bagel with her. This time she sat next to a girl who looked at her cheerfully and carefully. After a few minutes the girl looked up from the job classifieds, their eyes met and she asked Fiarette "What do you do?"

"Nothing exciting."

"I just broke up with this musician. He lost his job and he got so abrasive. I'm a social worker. Why don't I give you my card. I'm starting a group of people who suffer from Crohn's disease."

"What?"

"Crohn's disease."

"Is that K-r-o-n?"

"No, it's C-r-o-h-n — after the doctor who discovered it. It's a disease of the ilium; sometimes it's called ileitis."

CHAPTER 5

It is a rather pleasant experience to be alone in a bank at night.

Willie Sutton

Martin never gave up on his writing. He didn't do it every day but he thought about it most of the time. It was hardly something that could be timed or controlled or not allowed a life of its own. It was a guardian that brought with it an uninvited vulnerability that he would have been better off without. He was past fifty, heading towards fifty-five. He couldn't bear to feel the hard pulsing stir of life knowing he was losing his chance to conquer it, knowing all he had were the same old mindless tools. The plain undiluted possibilities of life scared him, plain but smug as a canyon. There could be vengeance, but, thankfully more often than not, there was affection with definition. He was seduced by time because time was the bullet. Time traced its effects; it hurt. He looked around him and saw people being noisy, exploding with volume, dancing and singing and making jokes and he wondered if they understood their lack of deliberateness. When he got too afraid, he did less writing, getting lost in chapters that never got off the ground and unable to bear the four walls. He wanted to be outside in the air, country air, mountain air, air with a sail to it, because lately the city air was losing its pull. Friends would telephone and he would try to be convivial, but once he hung up he lapsed into sadness. He thought about what it might feel like to be a writer famous enough to be known by his last name — an Updike, a Mailer, Fitzgerald, Faulkner. "Worthy," he thought — "not a bad last name."

Writing for Martin was about stopping time. "You have great physical powers and an iron constitution," his fortune cookie had said last night. Martin was starting to understand how really demanding writing was. At times it felt painfully subjective; he knew he had to be writing about himself. And then the tension would shift — he didn't know how he got there — and his words were positively objective. He had begun thinking that all his life he had fictionalized everything, every grudge, every building block, every disappearing act. He had watched; he had listened. A hundred others might have been there but it wasn't that important to them; they would hardly remember the memory much less be willing to reconstruct it. Martin smiled at the uniqueness of everybody's story. The combinations were endless. Everyone was part of something. Anything was liable to happen. Fiction, like life, knew no bounds.

Sometimes he got a brutal headache trying to flesh out dialogue — where do you stop? — how do you decide whether to leave people's words hanging in mid-air or keep them talking forever? He wanted to write without making judgments; he wanted to record and take a long time to make a point. He felt he was not a visual writer because he was impatient. He could certainly see the physical images clear and ironic — the black looks, the wrinkles, and the women close to tears. But he couldn't always sit still long enough to concentrate on that kind of detail because feelings took over.

Sometimes he would feel like creating, creating as opposed to reworking, creating as opposed to revising, shortening, widening and lengthening. He liked the way it felt to get the words down the first time around when they were raw and aromatic. He liked when they felt new even after they hit the paper. He could feel the process being born. Almost physical, it started at the top of his skull, his own reality being hoisted out. He never was able to know why the writing happened, but it always did. Words that a minute ago were inspiration became the words he wrote on long yellow legal pads. There was a fearlessness, a conviction, a connection to who you were. Nothing else got in the way; nothing else could. The feeling might be a face, a face in the sun, a yellow, golden champion, or a face in the wind, collar pulled up, wearing purple. People he had definitely never seen before wearing clothes he couldn't dream up. Creation was daydreaming. Studying it was work. He didn't want any bad guys in his work; he wasn't sure there was such a thing as bad guys. There were just people who never got a hint of glory, that's all it was. Lives could change suddenly; we ride cyclones. The will to live flounders. But for those who wanted it, survival was there. That was the part Martin enjoyed. That was the testimony he wanted to lionize, the weakened compromise he longed to make strong.

There were parts of his writing that Martin would wake up

eager to get to, characters he would put to sleep one night with a problem and wake up the next morning with a solution. He might bait his own anger and manipulate it for a character ready for indignation. In his writing Martin made use of everything he felt and he tried to make himself feel everything. Sooner or later someone would come along who needed to tell a joke, plan a murder, mourn a death, miss a beat.

Writing could be great theater; he would create a moment a person waited a lifetime to achieve. People came alive inside him at the most unpredictable times; the radio could be on about the magic of Macy's Men's Shop and a truck could be banging up a side street, but people inside his head were living and breathing and forcing their words out. Everywhere he looked, he looked for words. His writing would race, rarely meander. He would leave gaps in his thinking so he could get on with what he had to say. Sometimes his words sounded dumb, overdone, or just plain unnecessary. He would be afraid to cross them out because suppose he couldn't come up with more. He was often afraid of running out of words. It was hard work. He had to enchant the words before he could give them movement, before they could give him satisfaction, have them define something they had never seen before. And the stories, the plots; how much could you talk other people into doing? Raucous strategy didn't always work. Dense plotting wasn't always merciful enough. When would he be able to do better? He was not meeting the full challenge of his writing and that made him restless. And sometimes when he was least in the mood to pick up a pencil, something made him. How could he be sure of anything unless he put it in writing so he could read it back. He liked his memories and there was nothing like having them in writing. He did not understand what most people did with time; didn't this incisive awareness of time leave them disheveled? How did they keep track of it?

How could they know where they had been? Perhaps this fierce perception was his distinct luxury to enjoy. He wondered if writers should concern themselves with writing about "the same old thing." He wondered if he should write a western or a detective story. Whatever it was, it had to be good; he wanted it to count. He dangled his shoe, thinking up a name for a character and wondering why he always tried to make all his chapters the same length. How could they be?

In the *Sunday Times* was a photo story of Beirut and the war's aftermath, the bludgeoning of an entire city that might get reconstructed but whose history was gone. A lifetime spent putting it back together, a lifetime of sleep denied. He imagined living in Beirut and being part of the task ahead. He could feel the flat-out crisis of war. He had read that the wife of Dick Cheney, the Secretary of Defense, said her husband was calm inside; Martin wondered if that stillness was shock at the enormity of what might come next. Martin could not push the war out of his head. He had listened to the Senate debates on the presidential resolution to declare war on Iraq and the hugeness of it all. What of the patient course? When was it acceptable to speak out against war? No one wanted it but everyone thought it was necessary. The yeas were more than the nays: the use of military force if the President deems it necessary. The talk was of a vote of conscience. War is the least predictable option, a Democrat from Michigan said. No war is ever really over, he said. The idea that no war is really ever over filled Martin with indignation, an outrage that gave him strength. It felt legitimate; he accepted its validity and knew he should make fury an unalterable part of him. Immediately after the Senate debates was a home decorating show. They talked about flowers sharing space in a border garden and in another segment about decorating a room submitted the fact that there were actually three shades of cinnamon. He found he was surprised that so frivolous a subject was allowed to even be on TV when the country was so close to war. Maybe the war wasn't really so serious after all. If it was imminent, would people be on television telling you to pick colors you really enjoy?

At some point Desert Shield became Desert Storm and Martin thought this was actually very creative and wondered what branch of the government was responsible for naming battles. The electrical system in Baghdad was almost completely destroyed by coalition bombing within the first week. Allies would fly 110,000 missions during the war in a carefully orchestrated air campaign; 100,000 tons of bombs would be dropped. While massive air strikes continued, the world waited for ground assault and a bloody land battle. People would anguish and wonder why. Mothers with sons began protesting. An Associated Press photo was captioned "Technicians manning the Combat Engagement Center on the Battleship Wisconsin." There were charts in the newspapers of the major military units in the Persian Gulf. One was a group called the Gulf Cooperative Council, made up of local Arab forces and escaped Kuwaiti personnel. One newspaper said George Bush had "found his vision." People watched the war news like it was a movie.

Martin considered the fatal differences between offensive and defensive. All the students were against a war. Students were always against war. Their dreams are filled with social justice. No blood for oil. Rappers were doing songs on freedom "Peace to my brother, pearl of the future." People marched to the outcry of Hell, no, we won't go, we won't fight for Texaco. "CO" meant conscientious objector. Somebody sang "Don't wanna be a hero. Can't stand John Wayne."

Martin Worthy liked George Bush. He could remember

one specific moment when he started liking him. It was when Reagan was president and came home from the Gorbachev summit; Reagan got the red carpet treatment; the red carpet had been very visible, too, rolling forward from the exit door of the plane on afternoon television coverage. Nancy got flowers and they played the Star Spangled Banner. President Reagan mouthed the words; you couldn't hear if he was really singing or not. Nancy's lips stayed silent. Martin had always believed her smile. Kids waved flags from left to right to the tune of "Stars and Stripes Forever". The Air Force helicopter took off and the hands waving in air slowed down. Everyone looked proud of their President and thrilled to be an American. The television announcer called it vintage Ronald Reagan. George Bush was enthusiastic and, when asked about the royal treatment, smiled and said what's wrong with letting the other guy know how you feel? Martin thought that was great.

Before noon Martin went to the supermarket. He passed an old woman in the produce section buying bananas and could smell her strong perfume; he was sure her trip to the supermarket gave her a reason to put perfume on. Maybe she had run out of places to get dressed up for. She wore earrings and bright red lipstick. Then he noticed a young man looking at a five pound box of chocolates; the brand name was Zachary.

On the way back up the stairs to his apartment, Martin could hear the phone ringing. He hurried.

"Hello?"

"Will you accept a collect phone call from Andy?"

His heart stopped. "Yes, operator."

"Uncle Martin? I think my car was stolen."

"Where are you?"

"Madison and 34th Street."

He wondered what the hell he was doing at Madison and 34th.

"Just get over here, Andy, and I'll ask the questions when I see you."

"I think it had to be stolen, but I don't know why anybody would even want it."

"It's Friday, Andy. You can't park in New York City on Friday afternoon in midtown. It was probably towed. Just get down here."

"Oh, thanks," he said, "thanks a lot. How much do you think a cab might cost?"

"Never mind a cab. Never take a cab in midtown traffic. Just jump on a train; it's only one express stop. Get on any downtown west side train to Fourteenth Street."

"From Madison and 34th Street, is Fifth Avenue west of me or east of me?"

Andy was coming; Martin was thrilled his nephew trusted him enough to come to him in time of need and couldn't wait for him to get there. When Martin had been eighteen, there was no adult he would have entrusted his needs to. He couldn't remember being showered with attention by any of his uncles or aunts; they all had children of their own. He wondered if it had been important to them that he liked them. Had anyone loved him the way he loved Andy? He wanted to shower Andy, show him how much he loved him; here was a place to put his love, to be a good example.

Martin watched for Andy from his third-floor window; the sun moving west was a triangle across the street. He looked at the corner store which was now a travel agency with a small canoe painted black hanging up outside; in the spring it was full of flowers. He remembered all the things that corner spot had been over the years. An old man in the building told him it had once been a speakeasy. There were not many birds out today; he loved to watch the pigeons fly past his window.

Then he saw him strolling along with his hands in his pockets.

"What makes you think the car was stolen?" he asked Andy when he walked into his apartment. He listened to the boy's soft spoken potent intonations, the right voice for everything.

"I went into a store and when I came out the car was gone. But after I talked to you I told this policeman what happened and he said my car was probably towed, not stolen. He gave me this number to call." Martin wanted to hug him.

Andy got off the phone. "They told me my car is at 38th Street and 12th Avenue. Where would that be?"

"I'd better come with you. You might get lost." He was afraid someone might rob that beautiful calfskin jacket he was wearing.

Andy didn't say anything, just opened his wallet and starting counting.

"What's up?"

"It's $150 to get my car back."

"How much do you have?"

"About forty."

On the way to the subway station, Martin stopped at the cash machine. Soon they were crossing Twelfth Avenue walking towards a chain link fence with a sign that said that was where you reclaimed your car. Martin wished they were off to McSorley's instead where they could share a couple of brews and talk. He had a million questions none of which he knew he had any right to ask, but he was so anxious to know what it was like to be eighteen years old with the face of a poet. How did his day unfold? Did he understand the word capacity? Potential? Silver linings? But Andy was somber. His eyes had never been hopeful but now they were grim and said nothing.

Immediately inside the door, practically behind it, an old man with a small voice sat at a desk. He asked your name and told you if you had your license and registration in your possession, you could proceed directly to the cashier. But if you had only your license on you you had to go first to Information to get a pass, then to your car, get your registration and come back and pay the fine. Martin and Andy were about fifteenth on line and Martin wondered why a sign wasn't posted with the relevant details so the man didn't have to repeat them over and over.

Andy's registration was in the car so Andy had to stand on line for Information. There were two Information windows and three Cashiers' windows; at the top of each window were red and green stop and go lights. A yellow plastic chain kept people in a single line. People joked about having no license and no registration. Two guys were clowning around asking if you ran a red light at the cashier's window did you get towed again? Despite the one hundred and fifty dollar fine, most people were laughing. One guy announced that he had parked just minutes to run in and get a magazine; he was reading it now — it was *Penthouse*. The only person besides Andy who was dead serious was a guy from Yonkers who had a Porsche towed.

Andy got his pass from the cashier and while he went to the car to retrieve the registration, Martin held his place on the cashier's line. The room was starting to fill up; it was Friday afternoon about three o'clock. Martin wanted to ask if this was anybody's second time.

After Andy paid the fine he had to go alone to get the car. No one else was permitted in the pound. Martin walked back to the beginning, to the chain link fence which was the highest chain link fence he had ever seen. When Andy finally drove out he told Martin that besides the $150 fine, he had also gotten a fifty dollar parking ticket and three more tickets, one for a broken windshield, one for having no side view mirror, and one for not having his car inspection sticker on the windshield.

"Why didn't you put the inspection sticker on?"

"I never got the car inspected."

"Why?"

"It would never pass and I didn't have the money to get it fixed. It's just not one of my priorities."

Back in Martin's living room, Martin watched Andy finger the glass of wine. He balanced it in his right palm and placed his left palm over it. The radio was on about the war.

"Do you think people know how to make a truce, Uncle Martin?"

"Do you mean the war news?"

"The enemy is always dug in, isn't it. Somewhere there's always an enemy dug in."

"Andy, when I was your age, I hated when people said 'when I was your age.' But at the same time I knew for sure that when I did get to be their age, everything would turn out right. The answers would be in. The truth is that things don't turn out right. They don't turn out fair. And the right answers aren't the right answers for everyone."

"How do you know what to do?"

"I made my own rules a long time ago. I didn't set out to make them; they just happened that way. Slow. It's a slow process. I figured God knew my heart was in the right place and the rest would work itself out. What about you, do you believe in God?" Martin crossed his fingers out of sight at his side.

"Yes." Andy answered without hesitation.

"Then you'll be okay. You'll figure it out."

Later that night going out the door, Andy told him "You know when you think about the past and all your worst experiences? Well, that's what today will be, one of my worst experiences."

Martin wanted to protect him from indignities to come — far worse ones than having your car towed. He wanted desperately to take care of the boy and he was sad because he knew that he could not. He could not preserve for Andy forever the unqualified view of youth that sees cheerful construction while omitting many small details.

After Andy was gone, Martin sat down and wrote: "Dear Andy, being with you makes me realize how much I miss not having a son. I loved being with you. I love when you share your thoughts with me. I don't feel so much older than you do because I think emotions are the same no matter who they come from. Of course, I have some fears you may never have and you must have some I know nothing about." The letter was getting too serious. He felt good for feeling those thoughts but, ashamed of his needs and resisting sentimentality, ripped it up.

For days afterward Martin saw Andy's face, engaging and reflective, so young he had not learned how to engineer smooth mood changes. He had given the boy a warm hug when they parted. Martin loved him; he loved watching his expression change, slowly becoming commentary, never an easy grin. The affection that made him burst suddenly filled him with grief and the anguish of losing Elsa. He had been attacked by death and had stared at its crooked narrative until he willed it to lose power and float away. He did not know what he had created in order to understand death on its own terms, but it had worked. Death was a puzzle he had put in a box. He had packaged it into a rasping omission and sent it away. It had taught him to be generous, to tread lightly. Like being lulled by war.

The ground war began that Saturday night Greenwich Village time while Martin had become involved in a Rob Lowe movie. He could understand why people liked mindless comedies; here he was really wondering if Rob Lowe and Demi Moore were going to get married. The war news flashed on the screen just as Rob told Demi I love you. The war had begun. He felt jumpy, already an innocent victim, anxious because there was no one to talk to about it. He did not understand the war, the uneven crisis. The older you got, the more you were at the mercy of the vivid journeys of dimension. The thoughts stretch back farther. He thought of Andy; he was the youngest person he knew.

The next day he called him. "I thought maybe we could spend some time together under better circumstances."

"Maybe next Sunday, Uncle Martin."

"What time can I expect you?"

"Well, I don't know what I'll be doing Saturday night, so I'll just call you Sunday. But it would be in the afternoon."

On Sunday he hadn't heard from Andy and it was after eleven. He called him.

"Oh, hi. Good morning. What time is it?"

"Eleven — do you want to sleep some more?"

"Oh, yeah. Maybe just an hour."

"But you're still coming?"

"Oh, yeah, I'll call you when I'm ready to leave. It'll take me about an hour to get in there."

The day passed without Andy's phone call. That night Martin longed for an unforgettable sky.

Days later a scud attack was launched on Tel Aviv; the Philharmonic was performing and the audience put on gas masks.

Martin saw an old tape of a Malcolm Muggeridge interview on TV. Asked if the death of a child didn't diminish his belief in God, he replied that because such a death is so unreasonable it moves into the mystical and, instead of diminishing faith, enhances it.

This comforted Martin; his little Elsa was gone. Structure controls light and light controls color. His world had trembled with devotion in those months after her death when he tried to rearrange despair.

He returned to his typewriter and the story he was writing, thinking that what he needed was another character, maybe even two. He was unhappy with his writing, bewildered by plot and people with limited motives. He wondered how John Updike did it. How did he make up Rabbit?

From the street below Martin heard the single beat of a drum, then again, a disquieting lament. The sound moved, suffering, down the block, southeast, away from him, lingering and mournful.

He looked out the window and saw about twenty people walking up the street toward Seventh Avenue. He could not see their faces but he imagined them not all young. Shuffling single file, they wore big hand-lettered white squares of cardboard around their necks. He saw the back of one: it said CEASE FIRE.

CHAPTER 6

The first duty of a revolutionary
is to get away with it.

Abbie Hoffman

The papers reported on "Gulf weather today — a cold front accompanied by scattered showers will push into Eastern Syria and northern Iraq. High clouds will cover the sky in southern Iraq and much of northern Saudi Arabia.

Winds will be light from the south over the Persian Gulf." Maps shaped ground attacks. "Amphibious Marine forces could help pin down Iraqi troops along the coast of Kuwait."

"What do you want for Valentine's Day?" Martin had asked Fiarette the week before, when the Gulf war was twenty-two days old.

She knew that he would get her just about anything she might ask for. She wondered what kind of gifts he had gotten his wife — whether he had ever surprised her with a negligee or something extravagant made out of silk. She remembered the Robinson Crusoe book she had gotten when she was eleven and praying for a silver bracelet; that birthday ended up in tears. Now, more than twenty years later, she felt older by far but only part of the time. She would lie and tell Martin anything he chose would be fine with her.

On the morning after Valentine's Day, Fiarette looked outside and the sky was falling. She had been hoping for something pretty, not something expensive, not something binding, just something feminine. She got a goose. It was a cute goose, all right, with an orange beak and webbed feet and a blue and white tie around its neck. She especially liked the webbed feet; the goose's name was Gertie and she had wings. And later on when they got into bed, Martin lay his hand on her belly. There was an excitement knowing she was going to be made love to.

"What are you thinking of?" he wanted to know.

"Nothing."

He had taken her fingers and put them between her legs. She fiddled around but it wasn't working. She was thinking about two girls at work who were pregnant and happy. Another girl had gotten a single rose from her boyfriend for Valentine's Day and told everyone "I think by June my status will change." She could feel Martin moving from his place laying beside her; he was kneeling between her legs. "Spread your legs," he said, softly, gently, looking right at her, his hand finding its way between her thighs, his fingers opening her up, while she lay there and thought about the goose. She could feel tears in her vacant eyes and then began an almost exceptional mourning. She suddenly wanted to see her mother who had been dead for more than ten years. She wanted to see her desperately, to smell her, to embrace her engrossing complexities, to feel her wideness in front of her in one of those campy cotton housedresses she always wore, to be summoned by her presence the way you are only when you are a very small child. She wanted her attention at that moment in time the way she had wanted it right up to the day her mother had died. Her eyes brimmed with tears. Whenever they had their mother-daughter arguments, Fiarette was allowed to fight as hard as she needed, but it had to end there. That boundary was laid with unflagging precision. Get it out and get it over. The raw data was allowed to spill out and the fight would end, never to be mentioned again. Fiarette lay there, fastened to detachment; painfully alive made melancholy. She could picture her mother behind bedroom doors with the things she loved: her button collection or her collection of miniature dolls with painted lips and eyelashes that fluttered. She saved handmade lace and old doilies and confederate money and political pins and toby mugs and poodles made of hobnail glass. And when she got mad at Fiarette, which was often, she would leave notes full of angry handwriting that would always demand "What are you trying to do to me?"

Fiarette thought of those notes now. What had she been trying to do to her mother? She had wanted answers, speed limits, not a goose.

In bed with Martin something reckless was going on between her legs. She wanted so much to enjoy it, but she could not. It was an ideal setting, but she was not there, she was in pieces, thinking how much dying must be like falling, exasperated that she had been given a goose. All week long the *New York Times* had been hustling Valentine's gifts and shouting attention to passion: long stemmed goblets the colors of rainbows and chocolates meant to dazzle.

"You know what's wrong with this relationship? We don't discuss things," she started.

"What do you mean — we don't discuss things? We talk all the time." His fingers stopped.

"We talk all the time, but we don't discuss things."

"Like what?"

"Like did you used to hide things from your first wife?"

"Hide things?"

"Hide things. Like, did you ever, were you ever aware of trying to keep things from her?"

"What kind of things?"

"Things that you didn't want her to see."

Martin sighed. She was at it again, probing and trying to protect herself against some dark incursion, some attack that only she could see, even if the only way she could see it was looking back.

She wondered if it would be worth going to therapy again and paying seventy-five dollars to talk about not wanting the goose. And then she heard Martin saying "kiss me" and she did and the next thing she knew it was morning and she got up and touched the goose and found that she loved it. It was real white fur.

But her joy never felt legitimate for very long and soon she was blue again; there were no guaranties and she dare not change her expression.

And, sure enough, the next time they met, Martin ruined it by saying "Why do you smoke pot? Don't you know it's a drug?"

"Aspirin is a drug, too; at least I don't get headaches."

CHAPTER 7

You want to find an outlaw, call an outlaw
You want to find a dunkin' doughnut, call a cop.

From the film
Raising Arizona

Fiarette walked toward the homeless man who was selling stolen newspapers from a Met Food shopping cart; he had recently added *GQ* and *Self*. She saw him all the time and he always said good morning to her.

"Have a nice weekend?" he asked.

She smiled with her eyes down.

"Did you knock them dead?" His voice trailed off, "I bet you did." And then he raised it slightly as he called after her "Be sweet."

The first thing she saw when she got into the office was a message slipped under the lamp on her desk. "This 40-watt bulb is my personal property. I bought and paid for it. Thank you." It was signed by someone from the night staff. Fiarette wondered what this meant: was she expected to bring in a bulb the next time it blew out? Usually when the bulb burned out she just stopped using the lamp; maybe someone was mad about that. That day the staff were told via memorandum that from now on they were to use only initials when signing job orders.

They were not to write out either their first or their last name. People whose initials were the same — there were two JH's — were told further on in the memo how to distinguish themselves. Fiarette felt disheartened; next they'd be giving out numbers.

At work she had learned to keep her mouth shut. Secrets people thought were locked between them became whispered knowledge. So she stayed largely uninvolved. The most exciting thing that happened was Great Bear bottled water on every floor or someone trying to replace a Seiko watchband. Someone had called her opinionated at work. She had expressed surprise and the person had said, "Well, maybe opinionated isn't the right word; it's just that you always have something to say about everything." Fiarette didn't see where having something to say about everything was negative. She liked having a reaction.

Sometimes as soon as she got to work she felt sick; her stomach would ache like when she was in first grade. She wanted to be home watching *Regis* and *Kathy Lee — Live*. She wondered who was telling what on *Oprah*. She was intrigued by other people's involvements. At work she always felt she was going to get yelled at for something. There were few flashes of brilliance and no one was complicated enough to come close to crazy.

On Tuesday Fiarette went to a late lunch and sat in the company cafeteria and had chicken noodle soup and saltines and an apple. The other soup choice was Yankee bean which she had never had and wasn't in the mood to try. It was almost two thirty and all the silverware was gone so she ate with plastic. Most people were having lunch with someone. Almost everyone chose to sit at the tables facing the large rectangular windows that made up the north wall of the room. Two Japanese men talked the loudest and only one person, a woman in a navy suit with her hair in a bun, read a magazine.

Everyone else just ate. The weather had broken and was warm out but she was too depressed to go out of the building. She didn't feel she had the energy for even a walk around the block. Her eyelids were heavy. She had woken up in the middle of the night and had rubbed her hand over Martin's stomach. And stayed up alone, thinking, for an hour after that.

She saw a fat girl wearing a green dress and carrying a red lunch tray. It made Fiarette think of Christmas.

The Japanese men stood up from their table, bowed to each other and walked out together. They were quickly replaced by two more men carrying briefcases, one with suede patches on the elbows of his suit jacket.

The fat girl in the green dress sat down at the same long table as Fiarette, almost directly across from her. Fiarette tried to lower her eyes; she did not want anyone even looking at her when she was in such a bad mood.

But the girl sat there with a plastic bag from Record Explosion. "Marjorie Morningstar just came out on video. I love Natalie Wood; I think she looks just great, but I'm never very impressed with her acting; there's something wooden about her, you know?"

The girl started to unwrap a piece of taffy, popped it into her mouth, stopped a moment to read the wrapper and then started chuckling. She said to Fiarette "Do you want a good laugh?" Fiarette didn't answer.

"'Why are potato chips considered stupid? Because at parties they always hang around with the dips.' They have the best jokes in this banana taffy."

Fiarette was silent.

"I go to this diet club," the fat girl offered. "They tell us it's important to find something to laugh at every day. And to remember to smile even if no one else is around. Tonight is the anniversary show for Bugs Bunny. Did you ever see that cartoon about Bugs at the opera where he's dressed up like a drag queen? You know, I think Elmer Fudd lives for Bugs . . . just lives for him."

Fiarette smiled politely. The girl smiled back and got up and walked over to the rack on the other side of the cashier where they kept the potato chips. She took a bag without paying and walked back to the table. Fiarette watched as she sat down and ripped open the bag; Marabea wore a button that said "Don't confuse me with the facts."

CHAPTER 8

Anything becomes interesting if you look at it long enough.

Gustave Flaubert

Fiarette sat at her dining room table and rolled a joint. She kept her grass in the refrigerator and her rolling papers in a leather pencil cup embossed with a flower and the word Guadeloupe. She remembered the week she and Kary had spent at the guesthouse and how the hibiscus lit up the sky.

She took a toke and then two more. She liked the way E-Z wider rolling paper rolled best, but sometimes she bought other ones because she loved the packaging rolling papers came in. There was one called Cannabis Harvest with a picture of an old man with a beard and a wide brimmed hat. He was looking jovial. She wondered if he was high or if he was happy because he was a dealer. She decided that tomorrow she would go to the head shop — there were two she could think of within three blocks of her apartment — and look at the rolling papers and maybe buy four or five with the best artwork.

She took another look at the newspaper clipping she had torn out of yesterday's paper. It said "Go to Joseph for Family Peace" and offered a free prayer and a medal. She wondered why it had been placed in the Business Section. And as she got high, set in seamless slow motion, poking past the inanities, she was satisfied that all roads lead back to God. Her eyes were heavy and she grinned at the Guadeloupe souvenir. God had blessed her with those days when she and Kary applauded the power of their own radiance. Guadeloupe. They ate dinner late every evening at an open air place called La Fonda where Latins with heavy lidded eyes hung in the doorways and smiled at them. By the end of the trip they were mixing red zinger tea and brandy. Not much happened but it was fun, and it was one of the many trips Kary returned from thinking she was pregnant which she never once was.

The travel agent had told Martin the conflict in the Gulf was a war of nerves for anyone thinking about travel. Trip cancellation protection, like most insurance policies, didn't cover acts of war. Some companies had terrorist exclusions and would pay penalties on a cancelled ticket if a terrorist activity had occurred in that city in the last thirty days before someone was ready to fly. But Austrian Airlines had winter specials and Martin and Fiarette had decided on Vienna. Fiarette was thrilled about Vienna and thought about it all the time. She wondered what their hotel would look like and felt a tenderness toward Martin she didn't know she had. She hoped she would feel coquettish when they were on vacation. She was starting to feel foolish being sexy with Martin; after she slept with a man for six months, that happened. The minute they got into bed she would start thinking instead of doing. She amazed herself at how unmercifully long the list was of things that came into her head so unrelated to what the rest of her was doing. On this rainy Thursday she went shopping for the trip and bought three pairs of panties and rayon tie dyed pants and an oversized peach cardigan sweater with shoulder pads. She came home anxious to try everything on. She took all her clothes off and slipped the sweater on. It came down to her knees. She wished Martin could walk in right now. She wished she could plan it so it looked unrehearsed. She wondered why sex needed the appearance of spontaneity to be tantalizing. She remembered some of her more carefully constructed experiences. Deft, she had always been good at getting what she wanted, or, where diplomacy was called for, making the other person see it her way. She looked at herself in the mirror and was pleased with what she saw. The sweater had an open weave in front. One nipple was visible. She put her hands in the deep low pockets and swaggered. She wondered how other women looked at their bodies. Did they look over their shoulder like she was doing now? She knew Martin would love it if she would surprise him like this, but it seemed out of character for her, at least the character she envisioned Martin seeing. It would be easier to do it for a stranger.

She was so many people in her head. She was some of those people all of the time; others she didn't care for but understood came with the mix. She could not deny any of the parts that made up the whole. And she couldn't resist playing with delusions.

She only knew that these days she wasn't playing her favorite part. She wanted to play with Martin, sit on the bed and open her legs and invite him in. Beckon him from another room. Sit in his lap in a bath towel, outline his face with her breasts, her long red hair still dripping. These were the things she was thinking of when they were off to Vienna; this was the scope of her discovery.

On Saturday she became convinced it was time to clean her apartment when she looked all over for her sneakers and found them on top of the toaster. She tried to remember where she had put all those old towels that she had ripped in fours for the day she would finally get down to cleaning. Today she would refuse to be overwhelmed by the prospect ahead; she would try not to clean the same parts over and over; she would take things apart, unhook them, move them around. She would try to act interested and think of it as another chance at order. She would be systematic, starting in one room in one corner. She wished she could keep things neat, but she had no idea how people managed it. Do you start by putting away all the things that are hanging around but have a place to go and then take care of what's left over? How do you do it without getting distracted? The news on K-Rock was about a priest who had engaged in sexual misconduct and Fiarette thought about how big sins always started with one small wrong decision.

Her apartment hadn't been really cleaned in years. The heavy night tables in the bedroom had not been moved since they got there. She peeked behind them, down at the wrinkled wallpaper, and saw dust clinging to the wide molding. But to move the night table, heavy, marble topped, would mean to move the smaller table that was against the wall blocking it, past the fan which would have to be picked up. It would turn out to be the start of a major clean-up effort. She was thinking about independence and the importance of being flawless, but she rarely cleaned anything taller than she was. She looked around at all the things that were so hard to part with. What she was willing to throw out was insignificant; at the most it would give her a few inches of space and the only thing that would ever fit in that space would be more magazines. She would never throw out her *Rolling Stones* and found it hard to part with her *Vanity Fairs*. She stopped to read *The Log Home Lovers Design Booklet* from Greatwood Log Homes; one of the homes had a lower level with a private health spa with a sauna. It was called the Teton. Then there was the Walton which was a two story gambrel home. There were homes with names like the Virginia, the Elkhart, the Aspen; it was nice, but she threw it away. She didn't think she would ever be building a log cabin, although when she had picked up the folder the possibility seemed to exist. She didn't want to throw away any of her travel folders, no matter how old they were. She found a Christmas card from a friend who liked to believe Fiarette was on the verge of despair. "Take care and remember — this too will pass." She had enclosed a teddy bear bookmark that said Everything is bearable with Jesus. Fiarette tossed it. She flipped through a travel brochure from Suffolk County and saw the words GET YOUR BEACH SPACE EARLY. She decided to keep the cover page. It was a flock of flamingoes with sunglasses on at the beach, one poised close to the water with a tray full of long drinks, one cooking barbecue, two hamburgers on the grill, and another with a green wide-brimmed hat on her head. She decided also to keep the cover of a Smith and Hawkens catalogue that had come in the mail, a white Adirondack chair in an overgrown field of daisies.

She felt very grateful to God for being as happy as she was, even though she figured she was feeling that happy only because she was high. Pink Floyd was singing "Dark Side of the Moon", "You rearrange me till I'm sane." It was drizzling out, sixty degrees and still winter. Life couldn't have been more perfect. She decided this would be a great day for a facial and she put on a clay masque from Switzerland with red clover and white nettle.

Then, face tight, mask-like and mint green, she dusted the

oak washstand she had bought when she first moved into her apartment; she bought it from an antiques dealer who had moved to the Village from Amsterdam, New York. He liked her so he let her have it for fifty dollars. They had started having an affair when he told her he was in love with a black opera singer. She cleaned around a pottery vase someone had found in a graveyard in Cairo and wondered what it would be like to be a rock 'n' roll singer and do videos. She was more stoned than she wanted to be. Oprah's show today would be about kids who were addicted to Nintendo. She thought addiction could be okay: it made things stay important longer than usual. She started cleaning out the drawer and found a box with twelve sticks of musk incense. There had been a time in her life when she had burned incense every day; she used to take her incense burner with her when she took a bath. Her favorite had been Eucalyptus. It came in a box with hieroglyphics over it and liner notes that told about how the Egyptian slaves would steam the eucalyptus leaves over rocks and the aroma would lull the Pharaohs to sleep. You could always buy the best incense burners in Chinatown. Maybe when she went to look at the new kinds of rolling paper, she would get some new incense, too. Now she placed four sticks of the musk into the small brass Buddha, lit them all and let the scent lift into the small room. Queen was doing "We Are The Champions." She went back to her cleaning and found an orange plastic corkscrew she could not remember how to use.

She decided she wanted to live more elegantly. Not a lifestyle that would cost that much more, maybe just the difference between fifty and one hundred dollars. There were a lot of things you could get for one hundred dollars that you couldn't get for fifty and most of them were more than twice better. A lot of them in fact were elegant.

She moved into the kitchen and decided she would hang the white rubber wall grids she had bought at Third Street

Bazaar weeks ago. She got out the screwdriver and the hammer and pulled everything apart, but she couldn't seem to keep the screws in the wall when she tried to fasten them; they kept falling in the flower pots underneath the window and she got tired of looking for them in the leaves of the jade plant.

The telephone rang.

"Hello, Miss Streiter?" Fiarette's name was pronounced Street-er. This voice said Stri-ter.

"Yes?"

"This is Marlene Hoffman from Mothers Against Drunk Driving. Have you heard about us?"

"Yes, I have, Mrs. Bridges," and Fiarette's voice softened, saddened, almost as if she was, indeed, a mother against a drunk driver. "But, Mrs. Bridges, this is not a good time for me to talk. I just found out today that I . . . that I have cancer." Fiarette could feel herself sigh.

"Oh, I am sorry. I *am* sorry."

"Thank you, Mrs. Bridges. Thank you and good luck to you."

Fiarette hung up. She felt bad because she hadn't been gracious; she didn't feel like giving. She climbed in bed and lay there looking through the sleeve of her nightgown out the window. Absolutely nothing was getting better. She was searching for clarity, the flow of predictability that still had incalculable results. Was the rest of the world getting that different a message?

CHAPTER 9

Enemies forever, allies tonight.

An ad from Swamp Thing

Going through Customs in Vienna wasn't pleasant. The customs officer didn't want to be bothered stamping passports but the tourists wanted them stamped. Two people ahead of Fiarette asked for theirs to be stamped so by the time it was Fiarette's turn, he did it, although begrudgingly. Fiarette and Martin took the airport bus into town for four dollars. At the hotel they found a lobby full of schoolchildren on Easter break. Reception regretted it but they would have to move to another hotel because of these unexpected children. Martin tried to reason with them but the first hotel clerk, a young girl who stammered broken English, called the manager who promised them a hotel in a superior category. They would be sent by taxi and the hotel would pay for it. The taxi to the new hotel was driven by a chunky woman with dirty blonde hair who charmed Martin, but Fiarette was distant and disagreeable, even when she fell in love with the name of the street the new hotel was on: Mariahilferstrasse.

The reservations clerk who looked like Elvis Costello told them they would be able to stay there for probably only five nights and for their last two nights would have to move back to the hotel that had bumped them. He was apologetic. Martin begged, Fiarette flared. The reservations clerk said he'd see what he could do.

Their room with a small terrace was in a quiet corner on the top floor. The hotel that had bumped them sent over a bottle of white wine wishing them a happy stay — *Mit Bester Empfehlung*. The bed was delightfully hard with a white goose-down quilt that floated. Everything on television was in German except for Superchannel which originated in London. One night they showed an Amos and Andy movie followed by *The Great Dan Patch*, American, about 1952, with Gail Russell. Superchannel had world news and each country got about half a second. Fiarette continued to toss her clothes over the long low blonde table and Martin hung everything up.

Every day about three in the afternoon they had a wurst. They came in long rectangular rolls that were put on a spike to dig a tunnel through them; the wurst was stuffed in the tunnel, topped with mustard and ketchup, and then the top of the bread, pushed through by the spike, was put back on. On Saturday night they went to see *My Fair Lady* at the Volksoper. On Sunday morning they went to the Hofburg Chapel to hear the Vienna Boys' Choir. They were seated on folding chairs all the way up in a little room off to the side where they couldn't see anything and had to watch it on television. The mass was in German; the boys sang in Latin. On one side of her Martin fell asleep and on the other a Japanese man dozed off. After mass, they had tickets for the performance of the Spanish Riding School. There were two rings of seats, one eye level to the handsome oval-shaped riding hall, and the upper level where they sat. The music started and the horses padded onto the dirt floor and paraded elegantly into the hall to position.

Fiarette's favorite night was when they took the U-bahn to the Prater, the giant amusement park. The star attraction was the ferris wheel, Riesenrad, two hundred and nine feet high. They stepped into long red cars which were slid shut behind them and started the journey of just one long turn around while below a carnival flashed. After the ride they went into a beer garden and over tall glasses of draft watched a very thin man in a lime green suit with frizzy hair the color of ice dance by himself. A German group sang in English, mostly Beatles tunes. The final song was "Fascination" and Martin and Fiarette got up to dance. A woman on the dance floor smiled at Fiarette.

The next afternoon they went to Hundertwasserhaus, public housing by the artist Friedensreich Hundertwasser where the tops of some buildings looked like the Kremlin. The buildings were perched on a corner, their colors spilling off their sides onto the sidewalks. They were rose pink and yellow, bright blue and orange with stone work embedded with glass and mosaic, angled mirrors and fragments of pottery. You couldn't go into the buildings but you could use the ladies' room in the coffee shop where someone had scratched on the back of the door, "Art is everything."

There was Schönbrunn, the palace of one thousand four hundred and forty-one rooms where Maria Theresa was empress and Marie Antoinette was one of her sixteen children. Bonaparte's young son had died in one of the bedrooms there, an unhappy child who was ignored and had no friends; the guide said that the only friend the boy had was a bird, now stuffed, and still in a cage in the boy's room. The guide took them through dozens of rooms pointing out paintings of the family members and saying they really weren't a very attractive lot. Fiarette thought Marie Antoinette was the prettiest of all of them, but in most pictures everyone looked exactly the same. The grounds were romantic with trees pruned just like the guidebook said, "as tho some pair of heavenly shears had done them from above." There were Roman ruins, an aviary and a wonderful zoo. It was probably just about the time Fiarette was snapping a photograph of the rhinoceros that Martin's brother-in-law Spence was in the accident.

Every minute in Vienna Fiarette felt joy. The city was eloquent, its dignity intact, a fairy tale with intent and style. There was fluency and resonance and she felt blessed.

Emotions were tapped; she was responding. She had vigor. She was alive.

While Martin and Fiarette were waiting for streetcar #38 to Grinzing, a homeless woman came up to Fiarette. They were about the same age. A German man, noticing Fiarette's intrigue, began to translate. "My name is Verna," he repeated after the homeless woman as she spoke in German to Fiarette. "I live on the train. Anything you can spare, a piece of fruit you may be carrying with you, a piece of candy." Fiarette handed over her favorite scarf. She felt a desire to give; there was time for concern. She saw no turbulence in the woman's eyes; instead she saw something she wanted to have in hers: a curious courage. Martin was pleased because she took his arm walking down the street. And squeezed it.

On the plane home a group of political science students were going to listen in to briefing sessions at the United Nations. Their lighthearted chatter made Fiarette smile.

She needed something to smile at because coming home depressed her. It was over, again. Time was cutting things short, dealing a blow. She should understand disappointment by now; instead, pain was a crisis. Her left hand would ice up, like it was the first place that gave up her blood, and she was scared of life leaving her body for good.

Martin noticed her mood change on the plane.

CHAPTER 10

Q. In a previous column a writer referred to culminating a masturbation session with "a big finish." Would you elaborate further on just what this technique is? Is it harmful?

A. I believe the writer was referring to a climax, nothing more and nothing less.

From the column "Ask Isadora"
by Isadora Altman

"I don't confide in him," Fiarette was saying to Marabea about Martin, "he's too jittery to give me strength."

"You shouldn't expect another person to give you strength."

"I don't."

"But that's what you said." And then because she didn't want Fiarette to think she was incapable of understanding her needs, she added, "He could probably take care of you if you'd let him, but I know what you mean."

Marabea enjoyed the knowledge that Fiarette was involved with someone who was weak; now she could look to Marabea for strength.

Marabea had seen Fiarette in the cafeteria and had walked right over to her table. "I don't even work in this building but I still use the cafeteria," she said as she sank down. "Last time I even had a job, a real one in an office, I walked out. I bet you would think I got fired, but I walked out. They would have fired me if they knew what I did just before I left. I put all the gum in my mouth all over someone's typewriter keys."

Fiarette surprised herself by feeling saddened at this. Her

eyes looked it.

"I don't think it's funny what I did. I hardly ever find anything I think is funny." She picked up another french fry and shook her head.

"Why don't you think anything is funny?"

"I just don't get pleasure out of things. Even when they're happening to me, which is not too often, I don't feel much. I just go through the motions."

"You make it sound like pleasure is something that has to be learned."

"Somebody has to help it happen. I think there are a lot of people like me where things go on around them, but not to them, and they can hear but they can't really feel. And most of the people who make the rest of us feel left out think they're nice people; that's the mistake most people make. They like to think they're nice." There was silence as the last word trailed off.

"Don't you?"

"Don't I what?"

"Don't you want to think of yourself as a nice person?"

"We're not talking about me now. We're talking about you."

"You don't know me well enough to know whether I'm nice or not." But she knew that she had to agree. She was more and more aware of the things about herself that she disliked and the biggest one was that she wasn't compassionate.

"And," Marabea was saying, "most people feel they have to lie about it."

Indeed. Fiarette wasn't as nice as she used to be. She couldn't hide it and she didn't want to change it. Her feelings seemed to stop just short of caring, just shy of an intimacy that would let anything last longer than just long enough.

"I think I'll go home and get out my spy glasses. I got them in a Christmas grab bag one year when I was doing temp work. First I thought they were a toy so I was surprised when they turned out to be pretty powerful."

"What do you do with them?"

"I watch people. There's this girl in a building across the street who walks around half-naked. I see her get dressed from scratch and even though I can't see her face that clear I know exactly what she's wearing so I can recognize her when she comes out her downstairs door. There's about six or seven people on the street like that. I know exactly what they do when they're alone. I can see a lot. People think they're anonymous but they're not. With a good telescope you can see ten blocks away. When I see a naked person I just can't pull myself away. The fascination never wears off. It's great how most people never close their curtains."

CHAPTER 11

> "I'd like to order a blouse and pay by credit card."
> "Certainly. Just give me your credit number and expiration date."
> "Expiration date? How would I know how long I'm gonna live?"
>
> *Cartoon from a piece of Bazooka Bubble Gum*

Theresa would always remember the night she got the news about Spence's accident. She had just finished watching *Wheel of Fortune* and the answer to the bonus puzzle, where the prize was a trip to the Orient, was WISECRACK. The S-E-C-R-A-C part showed up but none of the contestants could guess it. Theresa wore a plastic cap over her head. She had colored her hair Loving Care medium golden brown and was waiting for the forty minutes to be up so she could rinse. She swept the wooden kitchen floor. While she had been waiting for Spence to come home, she felt nervous, more tired than she ought to be and jumpy when there was nothing to jump at. She had always been the kind of person where if anyone was even ten minutes late, she put the radio on for news of accident reports.

Spence had been standing on a Greenwich Village street that had six corners, wondering which way to cross. Out of the side of his eye he saw a big woman carefully set something down in an orange wire Department of Sanitation garbage pail. Her black frizzy hair was in a pony tail and she wore brown work pants and a black leather jacket. He looked into the pail to see what she had so guardedly deposited. It was a plastic coffee cup with the lid on. Before he could turn away, the cup exploded. He couldn't move. He clutched his chest and fell to the ground and everybody hummed around and said the coffee must have been a bomb or a very powerful firecracker.

Martin had just come home from the airport when Theresa called with the news about Spence who had already been in critical care for seventy-two hours. For the next few days Martin was haunted by the news. He imagined himself dying slowly, decelerating, getting smaller in the distance, waving a dim goodbye.

Martin's remedy was a return to his writing, a clean piece of paper where he could use some clout and suppress the chaos. Martin was as famous as he wanted to be. He was not after a luminous sprawl. It wasn't important whether anyone ever saw his words. Writing was what mobilized him. Every story had at least one part he tried to avoid; the necessary bridges always turned out to be sinister. He found it difficult to invent a rational path for things happening and spent hours probing at why major parts of life seemed to come out of the blue. Death reminded him that the best of plans was a valiant fragment. His writing reflected that. Life invented itself; he bracketed the anxieties. Each chapter was more a bitter outpost than a grand progression.

Fiarette was always after him to talk; he wanted to save his words for paper. She had a million questions about his wife, about his daughter; he suspected a lot of the time she was stoned but he didn't know how to tell for sure; she had a perpetual glaze. Sometimes she'd give it away by saying "I want a snack." He'd give her five dollars and she'd run down to the Korean market and come home with deep chocolate fudge tofutti.

The Gulf news had reached a point where the Mid-East analysts thought the United States would win the war but lose the peace. Every day the newspapers would list the latest daily numbers: how many Iraqi civilian deaths from allied air raids; how many Iraqi planes shot down; how many Iraqi soldiers surrendered; how many non-combat U.S. deaths. "Let's not fool ourselves," Secretary of State James Baker told the House Foreign Affairs Committee. "The course of this crisis has stirred emotions among Israelis and Palestinians that will not yield easily to conciliation."

There were the daily stats: allied sorties, the missing in action, the prisoners of war, allied planes lost, and losses to non-hostile causes. War. Men were shot down behind enemy lines, their worlds frozen rivers.

Martin was deeply saddened by the war; he felt bad about Spence; he was concerned about Theresa; he was worried about Andy. And he was always thinking about Fiarette. As far as he was concerned, it was no dime store romance.

"I love you," he had told her last night.

"But why?"

"You're resilient."

"Only a writer would say something like that."

He already knew that. "You don't want to talk about love, do you?" He tried to smile a seductive smile at her.

"If you're not getting enough air, I can open a window."

"Fiarette," he said, tired of the silliness of it, "if you're trying to come up with reasons why we shouldn't be together, I'm not going to fight you. You look sadder every day."

She glared at him. "I can't do anything. I can't do a damn thing. You can write. I'm not good at anything. I can't cook. I can't paint. I can't draw. I can't write, not even a two line poem."

"Did you ever try any of those things?"

"I don't have to try them. I would know if I could do them."

Martin, as he did more and more, said nothing. He did not know how to answer her, how to quiet her down, or how to match her passion. Sometimes he felt she was a natural disaster, more than he had bargained for, but it didn't stop his fondness for her lunacy and the way her face changed so many times during a day. He was madly in love with her. She inspired him although he was never able to tell her that. He studied her but didn't want her to know it. Since he met Fiarette, he had done little writing. The need was still there, but there was no coaxing and his days were not as vacant as they had been. She gave him something to do. In the beginning their relationship was that newness so right in reality it demanded no questions, no resolutions, nothing more than being there. Now whatever was left unspoken was what she craved.

"Maybe you could learn to make pottery," he offered, and bit his lip.

"You're making fun of me."

"Why is that making fun of you? Maybe you could learn to make pottery. I think you might surprise yourself and be very good at it."

"I told you, I'm not good at actually doing things."

He recalled her words and smiled. Was he obsessed with her needs? Did he want this relationship to be remarkable because so many had ended grimly? Perhaps he should liberate her to find the hero she grieved for. Maybe she would stop saying things like "I'm just doing time on planet earth."

Martin wondered where his life ended and hers began. More and more he wanted his own way and worried that his love was half the length it should be.

The telephone rang while Martin was reading *Travel and Leisure* about the Crystal Palace Resort and Casino Hotel in Nassau that charged $25,000 per night for a suite that comes with a robot named Ursula. Spence had died less than an hour earlier. Death was in the air, that common coming apart, a blank where once there was a being. Martin shuddered and begged God to keep everybody healthy. Not even a bad cold. The wake was at Reilly's Funeral Home where the boulevard became a numbered street next to an Oldsmobile car lot that had the latest models ready to go. Martin got there early and was directed down a flight of stairs to the lounge, a narrow L-shaped panelled room. He looked around: there was one settee, two settees, four settees, and many folding chairs. On one wall was a mural of a sailing ship and on another a highly polished plaque thanking Mr. Reilly for helping the youth of the community purchase and install a new basketball scoreboard. There was *U.S. News*, and two lamps with ceramic rooster bases. He remembered his mother using the expression "death warmed over" as in "She looked like death warmed over." He also remembered how she used to say "I have a headache to beat the band." He was getting a headache now, too, the trace becoming a tight knot, the comprehension that a death in the family means something is over for everyone else as well. Martin had been trying to put the war news behind him, to shake its brutal grip. Yet, the violence toward Spence was violence at its most monstrous, a shocking statistic close to home. One of the relatives at the funeral home remarked on how just about everyone was gone and then would come the cousins. Martin knew that when it was his turn, he must leave no unfinished business. He must put things in order, but when he wondered what remained to be done, the only answer was to strive for the self-improvement that would redeem him.

At the funeral home Andy looked lost. Protective of his mother, he stayed close by her side. Martin did not worry about his sister; he did worry about Andy. He imagined the boy feeling unconnected and somehow guilty for his stepfather's death. Martin still had a drawing Andy gave him of the afternoon they went to the circus — a crayon sketch of a wire figure on a tight rope.

Martin didn't know many people at the funeral home. This reminded him that he hadn't known his brother-in-law at all. A friend of his sister's came over and introduced herself; she was with her daughter who was telling someone how great it was to work at Mandees. Her boyfriend was there, too; he worked for a beauty school and tried to sell courses to people to study hairdressing. He was paid a salary of $150 a week, he told Martin, but would get $120 for each person he got to sign up for the course. He was trying to talk his girlfriend into quitting Mandees and going to beauty school instead.

In bed that night Theresa recalled a sermon where the priest had advised anyone harboring hate, unable to forgive, to read books on the lives of the saints. She reached onto her night table for the newsletter from church that past Sunday. "We experience the effects of loss at every level of our existence." She put it down and read Hints from Heloise instead. "I've read quite a few hints on reusing tissue boxes," it began. She looked again at the newsletter. "Grief is a response to loss, a cluster of physical symptoms and intense feelings. Because each of us is a unique being, we grieve in our own unique way. Our grief is valid, right and usually appropriate." She wished she had nothing to grieve about.

She went back to the newspaper. "I have a tip for you that was invented by my mother-in-law . . . "

And then the church newsletter: "Often we need to share the pain of grief, the shock, denial, disorganization and spiritual uncertainties."

The war in the Persian Gulf lasted forty-two days. Iraqis surrendered by the thousands. "We're not afraid," one young Iraqi soldier said, "we're just tired of war." When it was over, people worried that war would become acceptable as a way to solve problems. It didn't matter that the United States was the alleged victor; few saw any reason to celebrate. The old arguments came back: who was America to police the world and when would we learn to mind our own business. People called it outrageous that we could fund a war but not peace. Still lots of people thought you do what you have to do and hope for the best. President Bush's approval rating was at 86 per cent. The headlines boasted about "solid future," "well-learned lessons" and "Bush's afterglow."

A year later Saddam Hussein would survive and remain a threat. Eggs would be three dollars apiece, evidence of severe malnutrition would be everywhere, and children would play in raw sewage in Saddam City, a public housing project.

CHAPTER 12

We belong dead.

the Frankenstein Monster in **Bride of Frankenstein**

It was spring, the week after St. Patrick's Day, and winter no longer lingered. Sex was in the air with an early intensity and Fiarette was full of fire. When a man stepped near her, she felt it. She could barely think of anything else.

Sitting next to her on the subway to work that morning was a girl wearing a uniform from Dominican Academy, a Catholic school. She was studying notes for a class and Fiarette saw the words "vaginal foam and jelley." Jelly was misspelled. Fiarette remembered private school. The membership teas, the school newspaper, the *Quilt*, and the school song, "O! Ursuline. How well we hear your call, a-beckoning your tradition to all." Academy regulations came on tiny sheets typed up on an old manual typewriter with a ribbon that was never dark enough and stapled with a cover of construction paper, usually blue or white, the colors of purity. Stand in single file while waiting to purchase your lunch, do not play with your hair during class; she still had a bookmark one of her teachers had made for her. *Credo et Amo* it said. She recalled one of the most important rules: being in uniform meant that uniform was to be complete. No mascara, no nail polish, no lipstick, no hint of powder, no dab of perfume. She could see the forest green uniform and a close-up of herself in the uniform hat, a green felt baseball cap. She hadn't liked it then, but she wished she had it now. She would decorate it with a button of Moscow she had bought at the Russian Arts store. Now even the brown oxfords would be fun. How she had loved the dominant beat of those rules; in those days rules prevented chaos. They encouraged connectability. These days chaos and principle lived side by side and you could wear all the makeup you wanted.

On March 19, a Monday, at Fiarette's office, everyone found a Personal and Confidential envelope on their desk. Inside was a benefit statement stating the date of hire and normal retirement date. It was the projected annual benefit payable at normal retirement date, a number based on your present rate of pay, pension and social security benefits. Tomorrow was unresolved in her mind — she could hardly target the image. Fiarette's total estimated annual benefit was less than three thousand dollars.

The only calendar allowed at work was computer-generated. It didn't tell you a thing about quarter moons and seasons ending. Fiarette hoped for more gossip about the receptionist falling in love with the husband of the file clerk who relieved her for coffee break. Otherwise, it would be another boring day. About three o'clock Fiarette circled her first sick day on her calendar and walked slowly to her supervisor's desk and said she felt sick. "Really sick," she explained, practically limping, "feverish — here, feel my head."

"My hands are cold," her boss said, turning away, and Fiarette was sure she just didn't want to touch her. "Why don't you go lie down?"

"I'd rather go home. I think I'd better go home."

"Well, then, you'd better go home." Her voice was stingy

and she barely looked up.

The suggestion that she go to the ladies' room, as though her feelings were some temporary inconvenience, made Fiarette feel bad. In the ladies' room she would have to lie on a green plastic cot behind a folding screen where everyone would sit down, eat pizza and say, "What's wrong? Don't you feel good?"

On the way home an old lady in a wool cap looked into Fiarette's face and pleaded "Wish me a nice day." Fiarette wished her a nice day; she wished it to her twice. Coming out onto the street from the subway, a tall black man began walking almost beside her, but slightly in back of her, and she heard him say "Zoom, zoom, zoom, I just took it out of the sheath and stabbed her three times."

She actually felt sicker when she got home than when she had been at work. She was sure most of her unhappiness was because she worked in an office. It was something she did, but not something she wanted to become. It made her hostile because she was splintered. She tried to talk herself out of her bad mood but it didn't work.

Fiarette returned to work next day, March 20, a Tuesday. She was called away first thing from a rush typing job to fill in for someone who had been scheduled for training on the new software. He had a doctor's appointment and wouldn't be able to be there for the entire day's lessons. Fiarette had no time to calm herself down, no time to become receptive. She was not ready to learn wordperfect five point one. She was still uneasy with most of four point one.

The biggest change, the teacher said, was that the updated software was expressed in inches. There would be no more status lines that said Position 1, line 4, or position 10, line 35; from now on it would be 1.38 or 2.590 inches. She wondered what the name was for a fraction of an inch and decided that inchlets would be a good one. Someone else said he hoped they never decided to go to the metric system. No one was sure how to measure inches but the new manual came equipped with a plastic ruler. Now she knew things would be getting progressively worse. She had trouble telling which was the right margin and which was the left; it sounded ridiculously easy, but sometimes she couldn't think fast enough. She had to make the sign of the cross to be sure. The first hand she raised was bound to be the right. Everything on the machine, the teacher repeated, was in inches and increments of inches. Fiarette wondered if she should introduce her new word "inchlets." She was afraid she was going to start laughing; the teacher, a representative from the software people, went on about how the inches changed if you were typing in different pitch sizes. Fiarette had no idea just how far down the page line 3.67 was. One minute it was line 3.5 and then it jumped to 3.67 and then to 3.83. What were the numbers in between? She looked out the window onto the avenues stretching uptown with taxi cabs like yellow toys. She loved the way the buildings looked in the rain. Looking out the window was one of the pleasures of sitting where she did until the girl at the next desk decided she didn't want the blinds pulled up because it made a glare on her screen.

Fiarette took notes.

There are now relative tabs and absolute tabs.

Shift F8 will show you all the formats.

Alt E is the powerhouse macro.

She wrote down what she heard coming.

"Everything is inches," she wrote. Then she heard him say something about the powerhouse macro and that the tab line could be pulled up by typing Alt T. She looked at the tab line. It, like everything else, was expressed in inches. It was seven inches. She looked at the seven inches across the screen. Seven inches looked good. She thought of all the jokes about seven inches. Seven inches wasn't bad.

There was a short coffee break and someone told a story about her boyfriend's grandmother who had breast cancer and lost thirty-five pounds in two months. Her sister said it was because she never ate meat.

Hold down control.

Display pitch shows landscape.

Choose position by diagram.

Choose parallel with block protect.

She wondered if Martin was seven inches. He felt good in her. But he didn't feel as good as someone completely new. It wasn't the size, she thought, it was the surprise.

F-7, the teacher said. Exit. Close down the machines. It was time to go home.

Back at her desk was another memo. "If you are requested to transfer any new documents created in 5.1 to a secretary's machine and the new document uses any font other than 10 pitch, it will not print correctly." She didn't have any idea what they were talking about. The world outside beckoned with a louder and louder voice.

Early Wednesday morning she heard Sally Kirkland say on television that she meditated two hours a day and during that time reaffirmed her vow to be compassionate. Fiarette wished she wasn't so soaked in gloom so she could follow her example. Days ticked away in anxious isolation. She tried to read between the lines. It all stood for something but what. She wanted a mission that made her feel like the ad for The Royal Viking Line that says a truly great ship is something of a destination in itself. But she was on her way to work.

Every morning something was either stuck or broken. Today it was the "b" disc drive on machine number nine. Yesterday it was the message button on the telephone. It was difficult to feel comfortable when so many things were in need of repair. In back of her she heard her supervisor yelling at someone for sharpening red pencils and lead pencils in the same pencil sharpener; that would mean another memo on being cooperative.

People liked to talk about eyeglasses.

"These are just right."

"Uh, huh."

"I never thought I could wear round glasses."

"With your hair color, gold rims are good."

"Actually, these let too much light in from the side."

"I bet we have the same vision. Try these on."

Or about their doctors:

"I have a pinched nerve in my face?"

"What does the doctor say about it?"

"He says it's something that doesn't happen every day."

Or sending off applications to grad school:

"You should put your address at the top with more space around it," one of them said, watching over the other girl's shoulder as she set up her latest application. "You don't want to lose the benefit of having shortened the letter so maybe you should make the margins wider."

Work was dismal — the panic of repetition in an anxious internal landscape. Would she be fired if they knew the only way she knew which was bigger — three quarters or two-thirds — was to look at a measuring cup?

She had no real friends: the common denominator was work and for her that was a distraction. The only person she talked to was a recovering coke addict who told Fiarette that when she didn't wash her hair it looked great because it had nowhere to shrink. He was writing a paper about the sociology of aging and one of the headings was integrity against death. "The first phase is intimacy against involvement."

That night Fiarette lay in bed, wondering when she would attain the luxury of the overview, the wisdom that springs from retrospect. She lay on her back and looked up. The room was all lines, the windows long, the highboy floated and the square small panes of glass hung above the double doors. The newspaper folded at the foot of her bed was turned to a page 2 story about an icon at St. Irene's Greek Orthodox Church on 23rd Avenue in Astoria crying real tears. She wished it were true. She remembered lying on her bed as a child just the way she was looking up now, studying ceilings and thinking about walking upside down.

She began to play with the hair between her legs. It was not a sexual thing, but an aimless one. Her panties were already in the bathroom, where she tossed them automatically so she could wash them when she showered. Her pink corduroy dress was thrown over the chair. Soon it would get too hot for corduroy. That would mean half a year gone.

Almost nude. It felt good to be almost nude, just a big Miami Dolphins white t-shirt on. She got up from the bed and looked in the mirror. She was losing her looks. Her eyes weren't playful anymore. She didn't look anything like the woman she had been last year, the woman who was likely to follow a strange man down the street. She had forgotten how to look exciting. Martin was a solution to a problem. She loved the way his arms felt around her early in the morning, but the few smiles were rushed and she did not feel she was a conspicuous part of his life. She realized she no longer looked at men and she missed it, missed weaving passion and being indulgent. She had not forgotten the scent of the others.

The next day she quit work. She had not planned it. It, as more and more things seemed to, just happened.

When she was ready, she would find another job or another job would find her. Her job had infuriated her and it was great to be resolute.

Later that night Martin watched Fiarette. She had this habit of putting her hair into a completely new hairstyle while having a conversation with him; the talk was likely to be a subject that made her apprehensive and then she would pull her hair back with both hands, separate it into two ponytails, roll each one up, one just over one ear, the other behind the other ear, slip a haircomb through each and look wonderful. She had seen Kim Novak do it in *Vertigo*, tie her long ponytail into a bun. Tonight Fiarette was working her hair with particularly tedious detail. He knew something was coming.

"I quit my job today."

"Did something happen?" He was trying to stay cool.

"No, nothing. I just began to see possibilities."

"What kind of possibilities?" His chest heaved.

"The kind of possibilities you can't find out about when you have to be at work all day." There was a lot of silence until Fiarette said, "I heard on TV that if you want to access your childhood, you should try to write with your nondominant hand. They said you'll be able to express your anxieties freely."

"Did you try it?"

"Not yet. But at least now I have the time."

CHAPTER 13

Do not feel certain of anything.

Bertrand Russell

On a rainy Saturday afternoon Martin was listening to a talk show while he moved slowly through his apartment wondering which socks were dirty enough to wash. The topic was azaleas and hothouses, hearty versus pot plant and bringing them into bloom. It was the Garden Hotline and someone was on the line who couldn't remember what she was going to say. He turned it off and went back to thinking about Fiarette. He didn't want the persistence of her charm to paralyze him, which was what it was beginning to do. He found it hard to do anything but think about her. His thinking became disorderly, a failed road. When they weren't together, he wanted to know what she was doing, to peek in on her most secret moments, not to spy, but to achieve an intimacy that was denied him. What rooms did she linger in when she was alone? What did she wear? Where did she sit and how? And for how long? Did she daydream?

Martin recalled what Fiarette had asked him last night. "Where do you get hot first?" He was amused that this what was going on in her head just one day after she had quit her job. As far as she was concerned, quit had meant final; the job was history.

He had been watching her, sitting on the arm of the sofa, studying her from behind, watching her ass. He felt gluttonous but ashamed of his excesses, so he averted his eyes and then snuck another look from the corner.

That was last night. She was gone now but he was still absorbed with her. Good art has to do with the material but great art has to do with the idea.

About ten that night, while he was shaving, the telephone rang.

"Uncle Martin?"

"Andy."

"Hey."

Pause.

"How are you?"

"I'm doing good, Uncle Martin. Listen, I have your money, you know, that you lent me for the car, but if it's not going to be a problem, I'd like to send it to you in two weeks instead of now because my rent is due and if I don't give it to my mom, I'll be at your door with a suitcase."

Martin was thinking he might like that very much. "That's fine, Andy, two weeks will be fine."

"Thanks. Hey. Thanks a lot. And thanks for the article about the comic books."

"Was there anything good in there?"

"I didn't get a chance to read it yet."

"Andy," Martin began, not knowing what he'd say next but not wanting the boy to hang up. He savored his sound, the sweet husky voice. "Andy, how're you doing? You know . . . really doing?" There was silence. Had he gone too far? "Don't think of death as losing something." The words came naturally.

There was still silence but it was not threatening.

When Martin hung up, although he was not smiling, he was gratified the boy had remembered his phone number. He had wanted to preach without sounding like a preacher. Don't think time is forever, he had wanted to cry out. You won't believe how it gets used up, how the past piles up and the future shorts out. He wondered if, given the opportunity, he would fill Andy's head with his own bulky beliefs, with an unremitting cry that could put the fear of God in you. The universe was planted. Go for it.

But it was different with Fiarette; he didn't want her to do it all. He couldn't understand why she always wanted more. Her life was full enough. He smiled at his vulnerability.

He picked up the phone and dialed her number.

"Hello."

"You sound all out of breath."

"I'm doing aerobics to a Jody Watley video but I shut off the sound and I'm listening to a Red Zone tape that I bought on Astor Place." The sweat from doing Jody's moves was dripping on her. "What are you doing?" she said, wanting to get sweatier.

"Writing, trying to write," he said. Behind him the porn star on the TV interview show was saying, "You got to be able to read a page of dialogue and maintain an erection at the same time."

"What are you writing? Are you writing about sex?"

"That's not easy to answer."

"You don't want to tell me?"

"That's not it. I think passion is a better word for what I write about."

"Passion *is* sex."

"It can be."

Fiarette wanted to hurry off the phone. She was into her own thoughts about how she used to jam her moods into dancing until daybreak, in the days when she believed sensitive was any guy who went to a disco.

"Fiarette," and he knew his voice hesitated, "what do you think you'll do now that you're not working?"

"I don't know yet. All I know is I'm not going back — the weather's getting too nice."

"What do you think about spending a couple of months in the country?"

"The country?"

"Upstate. Kate and Teddy's place, the ones with the Christmas party every year. They bought a house up in the country and now they want to rent it."

"How come they want to rent it?"

"I don't know — I think they're going to Portugal or something."

"All summer?"

"I don't know," he sighed. "Fiarette," he said, snapping her to attention, "What do you say I take the house for the summer — we'll just move everything up there for awhile, get away."

"It sounds good," she said.

"Really?" he said, honestly surprised.

"Really." She thought about it some more. "Actually, it sounds great." She was smiling. "When will it be?"

"Oh, another couple of months at least. You're not going to change your mind, are you?"

"No." She didn't sound convincing, but Martin blamed his qualms on himself.

"It'll be good for Andy, too," he said.

"Andy?"

"Andy. My nephew."

"I know who you mean, but what does he have to do with it?"

"I think he needs a break from his mother. I know my sister. I think her relationship to him is going to change now that Spence is gone, but I'm not sure how. She's either going to smother him with affection or nag him to death."

"Or ignore him," Fiarette suggested.

Martin was touched at her contribution. "Ignore him. That's an interesting angle." He didn't think she could be right but he'd give it some more thought.

"That would be the worst of all," Fiarette added, "if she ignored him."

CHAPTER 14

Don't hate your enemies — it clouds your judgment.

From **Godfather III**

A clear blue framed the city, a beautiful day when even car horns sounded no more showy than a song. Marabea spent it watching Wicked Woman Day on TNT. Her day began at 10:00 a.m. with *Wicked Woman* (1954), Richard Egan and Beverly Michaels. At 12:30 was *The Shrike* (1955), Jose Ferrer, June Allyson. At 2:30 it was *Ada* (1961), Susan Hayward, Dean Martin and Wilfrid Hyde-White. She sat in front of the television set wearing a XX large red T-shirt from the sporting goods store. Around one o'clock she warmed up some pea soup and ended up spilling it all over her T-shirt racing back to the TV where the commercial had ended sooner than she expected and the movie had begun. She went into the bedroom to take off the T-shirt and change to something clean and looked at herself in the mirror. She couldn't believe how fat she had gotten and how fat she was letting herself get. Tomorrow she would start taking dexatrim; she had squirreled away some of the little red pills in old film canisters. She was never able to stay on the program for the full thirty days it took to finish the pills. They made her listless and lackluster, and, depending on her state of mind, could deepen into exhaustion and indifference. After a week or two the diet pills stopped working. She had seen an article in a woman's magazine while she was vacuuming someone's fake oriental rug. "Why despair when sadness is sufficient."

She grabbed at the fat on her body and felt empty. She thought of Beverly Michaels in the film this morning, *Wicked Woman*. Beverly Michaels exploded with sex; her hair was platinum and she was as tall as all the men in the film. She walked the way movie stars used to walk in the fifties, her body rolling in power. She wished she could look in the mirror and see herself in Beverly Michaels' body. For a moment she thought if she wished hard enough, it would really happen: she would look in the mirror and be thin. Long, thin perfection. She felt panic. She was so far away from who she wanted to be; she would have to devote such time and hard work and she knew she was not strong enough for the job.

She thought of the girl whose apartment she had cleaned yesterday; she wore yellow, the yellow of sunshine, a short yellow cotton sweater with big shoulder pads with her belly showing. She hated her; she could feel it then and she could feel it now, a grisly bitterness. It was a distinct threat to her safety. It looted her freedom.

Where did her meanness come from? She felt a conspiracy towards the rest of the world. If someone she knew was going away for the weekend, she hoped it would rain. If people sneaked, she wanted them to get caught. And if they sneezed, she found herself wishing they would get sicker. Sometimes she would get mad at a state, for God's sake, a whole state, a state of the United States. Like when California was having a drought problem and she was glad it didn't rain because someone she was jealous of had moved out there and she wanted her to suffer. It was her nosy neighbor's daughter, who not only moved to sunny L.A. but was doing really well as a script girl at a movie studio and even went to the same gym as a couple of movie stars. Face to face with her anger, Marabea wanted to snicker at it but she knew better. She knew she was being buried in it and that it was a significant meanness. She had never been popular, scarcely been noticed, hardly been liked and she searched for a genuine sense of place. She could not see herself as pompous but she felt no bond with anyone. The rest of the world were the imperious ones; she was the one who suffered. They had betrayed her.

She wondered if there were any new diet clubs in *New York Press*. She glanced through it and stopped a few pages from the back where the pages were filled with "Oooh! Yes! Call me now. Live sexy hot talk." And "only eleven cents a minute for cheap thrills." She looked at the sex classified, about fifty ads, with words like "diamond finger." Then she saw

> Busty female wanted
> for semi nude light apartment cleaning.

She dialed the number. It was an answering machine.

"Hello," she said, "My name is Beverly. I think I have what you want." She sat in bed with the newspaper in her lap and skimmed the ads, pulling lines from them. "I'm a hot gal, nasty and cheap. I'll make you feel terrific. Call me soon." And then she happened to see the 1-800-TRY-ASIA ad and ended with

"We can eat sushi together." She used her own telephone exchange and made up the last four numbers.

Maybe she should put an ad in *New York Press* to clean apartments. She turned to the classifieds and looked. There were sixteen ads under CLEANING and one person had fourteen years experience.

She was struggling with her food, never able to feel full. It was so hard to say no. She was going to her first acupuncture treatment at seven o'clock.

The acupuncturist's office turned out to be on the eighth floor of a building on Lafayette Street, south of Prince and almost in Chinatown. Chinatown was spreading north so maybe it was already there. Marabea had seen the ad in one of the newspapers, *Free Spirit*, handed out free at the health food stores. The elevator in the old building frightened her. It stopped at floors it wasn't supposed to.

In the office, an L-shaped space with folding screens, a Chinese man was boiling water in an orange hot pot on the wooden floor. Marabea walked in and noticed that the only place to sit was against a light gray wall that looked newly painted on a very narrow bench padded in black leather. She wasn't sure she would fit.

"Are you the teacher?" he asked her, standing up with the hot pot in both hands.

"No."

"You have the trouble with the smoking?"

"No." She wanted to scream: can't you see what I'm here for? She felt bigger than ever. She had gone into the deli for an orange and come out with a cellophane bag of Swiss stars, tiny cookies shaped like stars with a soft drop of chocolate in the middle that melted in her mouth. She was excited because she had never had them before. The usual price was $1.49 but it had a "Special Today 99 cents" sticker on it. By the time she got to Lafayette Street the cookies were gone.

"The weight will come down," he said, pushing his palms slowly downward, like in a ballet.

He led her to a table against the wall with a sheet of paper on it. "Take off your shoes and socks." She lay down feeling her heartbeat in her ears. "Disposable, see?" he said, holding up needles in a sealed pack and told her to close her eyes. She tried not to look when she felt the needles. Several needles. A few in each foot, each ear, each hand.

"How long do I have to stay like this?"

"Forty-five minutes."

She rested her hands on her stomach which had never felt bigger. She wanted to see what time it was on her wristwatch but she was afraid to look. She didn't want to see the needles stuck in her hand. She wondered how long each needle was. They felt very long. She was afraid to move her head for fear the needles in her ear would go in too deep, right into her skull. She felt she was being punished. She heard him come back into the cubicle.

"Do you feel anything?" he asked.

"What do you mean?"

"In your ear."

"Like what?"

"Electricity."

She was beginning to feel a tingling which became a delicate shock that rang like a bell, first in the right ear and then the left. He adjusted some knobs and left the room. Now she could feel the exact placement of each needle and her ear lobes were vibrating. She could see thin wires attached to her ears leading to some ambiguous machine. And at one point in the next forty-five minutes she heard herself snore.

When it was over, she lay there while he removed the needles, sometimes two at a time; she could feel them being pulled out. It was only when all of them were out that she was able to calm down.

He gave her another appointment, telling her she had to come twice a week, and she walked out of the office sleepy on her feet.

CHAPTER 15

Humphrey Bogart is supposed to have told Frank Sinatra that the only thing you owe the public is a good performance.

Outside Fiarette walked aimlessly. Someone had thrown away a stack of eight by tens on good stock photographic paper. They sat on top of a black plastic garbage bag next to a rolled-up folded-over carpet. All but two were of the same couple. He wore glasses and a boat-necked T-shirt and she wore a striped blouse with a bow at the neck. They were holding hands and smiling in all the pictures. Only one was of him alone and only one was of her alone, with much longer hair. Nearby on the ground lay strips of exposed film.

In front of her was a couple wearing canvas rain hats; the woman's voice was deep as a man's. She was laughing and saying something that sounded like "Be bofa ba that."

Fiarette stopped in the Middle Eastern café where they listened to folk music and in the card shop where the Spanish woman listened to opera.

The Indian outside the shoe store looked straight at her and said "Ladies' shoes on sale inside." Fiarette shook her head. "So don't," he said.

She stopped at the flea market on the triangle of streets at Astor Place. One guy, taking long swallows from a bottle of red wine, sat on the ground in front of a blanket of mostly shoes and frames. Someone told him "Paint it up — somebody'll buy it." He was talking about a frame with a paper picture in it and said he had already made sixty dollars that day.

"I don't have to ramble out," a guy, rapping, passed her. He wore a T-shirt with a picture of a gun pointing East: "New York City. It Ain't Texas." A paperback stuck in his back pocket; she could see George Orwell's name. The guy's swagger made her think of Alex, that mess of courage with a prayer. The last time they had taken a walk to the East Village Alex had remarked that more and more of it was missing. Gem Spa was gone and the big dark record store around the corner. The Gap was there now, and restaurants like Nizan's Indian Cuisine and Café Rakko. Stamped in green on the sidewalk were the words THIS IS A TROUBLED PLACE. Across the street someone had started a mosaic collage with the message in tiny white stones. WE THE PEOPLE. The words were set in cracked plates, cracked mirrors and the top corner of a mug that said "Justice for All." There were red stones, plaster heads of people and the green glass bottoms of Seven-up bottles. On Dinkins' old campaign storefront there was a sticker: Let's Go, Mets. The words SHUT DOWN WALL STREET were scribbled next to it.

A tall girl with a long shiny black pony tail sashayed past her and then past three men strolling just in front of her. Fiarette could hear the guys talking about the girl's ass. She wished she could hear more without being obvious; she liked to hear men talk about women's bodies.

Fiarette walked into the 23rd Street Y and up three flights of winding marble stairs to the ladies locker room. The lady who had the locker next to her was putting on blue gym shorts over a lily white girdle. The woman gave her a big smile. "My boyfriend moved in last Friday. He had so much stuff but at least I talked him into getting his two cats adopted. He's a real sweetheart, sixty-three, has all his hair. But he's overweight." She patted her stomach. "That's why I've put on some weight, because of eating with him." She closed her locker door. "I'm taking stretch from five-thirty to six."

Fiarette pulled a pony tail holder around a hunk of her hair and walked off, towards the ladies' exercise room, wondering why people need to live together. The woman kept talking. "My last boyfriend fooled around right in our own backyard." Fiarette pictured someone making love under rose bushes.

In the exercise room she got on the bike. While she pedaled, she looked at the ads for Guess jeans in *Vanity Fair*. The ads were printed on heavier paper than the rest of the magazine. She studied the models. Her favorite was the girl gazing out a door down a street as though she was waiting for a lover. A no-good lover. She wore tiny panties and a scooped bra. She had no hips and a perfect belly. Fiarette pedaled faster. In the next picture the same model showed up wearing bracelets up to her elbow and both her arms were around a guy who looked French. They were on a motorcycle and you could see the wind in her hair.

She wondered if Martin would ever read the book she had given him. It was *House of the Sleeping Beauties* by Yasunari Kawabata. She believed Martin loved her but he wasn't able to make her feel valuable. He didn't make her feel as though she was able to contribute anything substantial to his intellect. She decided he would never read the book. He wanted to choose his own reading. She wondered if he liked to read at all. He seemed perfectly content watching television as long as it had a fierce narrative. She wanted desperately to leave her mark on something he did or something he thought.

Fiarette struggled with the fifty-pound weight on the shoulder press on the Universal machine. She noticed the top weight was 250 pounds and was awed at who could really lift all that weight. When she walked into the gym, her intention was always to stay for at least an hour and a half, but she never stayed that long. Sometimes it was the noise; chatter distracted her. She had tried headphones with old disco tapes but the headgear was awkward when she did certain exercises. She had tried clipping her Walkman onto the waistband of her gym shorts but the stretch from her waist back to her ears was too long and the Walkman would pull loose. Working on the weight machines made her restless, too edgy for a sauna, too distant for aerobics. She wondered if the guy who checked memberships paid attention to how long people worked out upstairs. She had been here less than thirty minutes and some girls seemed to stay all afternoon. She could tell by the way they talked to each other zigzagging around in the white terry cloth bathrobes the gym supplied with a full privilege membership. "I went swimming this morning and I'm going up to the track now." It was after two. She was done.

★ ★ ★

Outside the sunlight lit up the street. She went into Woolworth for a new shower cap. She passed a rack of coffee mugs: pink for girls and blue for boys. All the names were Spanish. The girls: Blanca, Dulce, Iliana. The boys: Abuelo, Benito, Diego. She thought of all the Spanish boys she had been to bed with and wondered if sex had to be wicked to revitalize.

Outside she saw a bag woman with matted hair and wounded awareness. Her stockings were falling down. She had five shopping bags. There was no way she could manage them all, so she put three down, went back and carried the remaining two twenty feet forward, put them down and returned for the first three which she carried twenty feet past the other two. Four were white plastic and the fifth said Ralph's Paramount. On the next block Fiarette passed some people in white robes with sandwich boards around their necks pushing resistance news in eight languages, French, English, Spanish, Urdu, Swidish (Swi, not Swe), Grman (the "e" was missing), Arabic, Italian. One wore a red T-shirt that said Christ Satisfies.

Maybe it was Martin's hands; maybe they weren't rough enough. They were the hands of a man for whom sex was less a passion than humble disinterest. Maybe she should stop comparing everything to Spanish boys. Fiarette walked into the book store where the security guard started to staple her shopping bag shut. "Do you have to staple it?" she asked. It was a pretty shopping bag, one she wanted to keep and she didn't want it full of staple marks. "Can't I just leave the bag here?" she asked him. "No, ma'am, I may have to chase a criminal and your purchases would be left unguarded."

She began to wonder how much longer she would live and at what season of the year she would die. Autumn was her favorite and she didn't think she would like to die then. She walked into Washington Square Park and strolled slowly around the fountain; when the weather warmed up, it would be roaring. She thought of the fountains in *La Dolce Vita* and decided she would rent the video. A girl walked by wearing bright lipstick and beaded sandals. She looked about nine. Most people looked like they were from the midwest or New England or anywhere but New York. She saw a kid in a sailor's cap and a girl with a T-shirt that said Computer Illiterate and Proud of It.

Back on Eighth Street she read a billboard. Someone had chalked SELL ME A GOD and a group called The Beautiful were appearing at the Lyric Theater in Times Square. Appearing on Houston Street East of A were Gamma Rays, Anastasia Screamed, Chuck Prophet, The Shams and Hello Strangers. A taxicab turned the corner slow like a dance step. Certainly time was passing. She could feel the minutes bare in their bounty.

In Bagel Buffet Fiarette ordered tuna fish, lettuce and tomato on a sesame bagel. It was ten cents more than yesterday.

She sat down at a table for four with a woman and her son whose name she soon heard was Sammy. "And I have another birthday present for you, Sammy." It turned out to be tickets to the circus. "And dad and I will *both* have breakfast with you next Sunday." The little boy didn't say much except that he wanted a blueberry muffin only and no, he didn't want French toast. The rest of the time he sang, a one note song that sounded like a nursery rhyme.

"That's a great song," his mother told him. "Did you make it up?"

"No", he said, "I just know it."

Then she got involved watching a delicate lady with hardly any shoulders. Her eyeglasses were bigger than her eyes, which were blue. With the tip of her fork she tugged at the extra dough in the center of her bagel, pulled it out and buttered it separately. She lay aside what was left of the bagel next to a napkin smeared with lipstick. She was talking across the table to a boy with an MTV cap on; she looked too old to be his mother but was probably a relative. "How's your allergy?" she said. "Have you outgrown it?"

"Hi."

Fiarette looked up. Someone was smiling at her, someone she was sure she had never seen before.

"Don't you remember?" Her frizzy black hair was in a pony tail. She wore brown work pants Fiarette was sure she had seen in Hudson's Men's Shop windows.

"I don't think so," Fiarette said.

"The cafeteria. We met in the cafeteria of that office building on Park Avenue. We had lunch together."

The girl sat down at Fiarette's table with a tray full of food.

"I don't know what to do. I've been gaining all this weight. I just got into this thing of being hungry all the time."

Marabea liked the way Fiarette looked, just the way she would have wanted to look, lots of color but subdued, cool but not stylish. She wanted Fiarette to pay attention to her.

"Have you been to that cafeteria lately?"

"No, as a matter of fact, I haven't."

"My name is Marabea." She smiled.

"Hi."

Marabea was disappointed when she didn't say her name but was determined to get it out of her. "I've been coming here ever since I moved to the city about a year ago. I pulled a disappearing act back home; just sold everything I owned and disappeared so I could react to a different environment." She wished Fiarette would ask her where she had come from. She looked down at her food and was ashamed of how her plate overflowed. "I'm always hungry." She started to eat. "I was very fat, then very thin and now I'm getting fat again. But this time I'm keeping my name."

"What do you mean — keeping your name?" She had to ask.

"My real name is Marilyn Beatrice but I always think of that as my fat name. When I got skinny I changed it to Marabea. Doesn't that sound like the name of a thin person? But I'm going to get thin again so I'll just keep the name. What's your name?" She had to know.

"Fiarette."

"You know, you're going to think I'm crazy and maybe I shouldn't even tell you this. But I had a dream about you last night."

"A dream about me?" Fiarette had her doubts but her eyes were glowing.

"It was a wonderful dream. You were skiing and you wanted me to take pictures of you. I was standing in the snow at the foot of a great mountain and was shooting pictures, one after the other, of you coming down the slopes."

Fiarette was enjoying the idea of being such an excellent skier that she was masterful enough to challenge mountains. She wondered if she should tell the girl she had never put on a pair of skis in her life.

Marabea had finished her food and had only a bagel left that she wished had more cream cheese on it. She watched Fiarette scooping away gobs of cream cheese from her bagel and putting them on the side of her plate. Fiarette saw her looking. "I'm not going to eat this so take it if you want," Fiarette said, moving the cream cheese toward Marabea. Marabea laughed and dipped her bagel into it. "I bet you never have to go on a diet."

"Oh, everyone always wants to be thinner."

Marabea felt hurt. Even this girl, a tall skinny inspiration, wanted to be thinner; she must think Marabea was a pig.

Fiarette studied Marabea for the first time. Her face was round, baby faced; she twinkled more than she glowed, but her eyes were angry. She had taken off her black leather jacket.

Marabea was plotting. First she would be polite. "I hope you don't mind if I sit here," she said sweetly, looking as though she was ready to pick up her black leather jacket and move to another table if she was at all in the way. "Oh, no," said Fiarette. Marabea quickly felt secure; she had just about shamed the girl into paying attention to her. The rest would be easy.

"I'm sorry I'm not such good company. I just quit my job and I never thought I'd say this, but I think I miss it."

"Why'd you quit? Was it the place with the cafeteria?"

"Yes, it was in that building. Why'd I quit? I know why I quit. I quit because I got scared I was spending too much time indoors. Can you understand that?"

"God, yes," Marabea said.

"I wanted to make something happen and I couldn't make anything happen there. But now I feel lonely. There are people there I keep thinking about, wondering how they're doing. There's nobody I can't do without but it still feels bad. My best friend died last year and I still can't believe she's not here. I keep thinking I'll turn a corner and she'll be there. You just don't expect your best friend to die. You know?"

Marabea thought the best thing she could do was listen. But she said, "I never had a best friend. Maybe that's what's wrong with me." She hoped Fiarette would ask, "What's wrong with you?" but Fiarette continued talking about her friend and Marabea wondered if she had been thin.

"Kary tried to teach me to be more spontaneous — she was always saying, let things into your life."

Marabea wished she didn't have to know her name.

"She'd be real proud of me for quitting my job."

Marabea saw Fiarette smile and took it as a clue. "I don't even know you, but I'm sure you did the right thing. You can always find another job but life doesn't give time away."

Fiarette smiled at her. Maybe she did understand. Marabea felt her warming up.

"You know what happened?" Fiarette continued. "I realized that my boyfriend might end up being the last man I'd ever go to bed with. It should have been a comforting thought but it didn't make me happy. And that scared me because I can't imagine myself cheating on him. So the whole thing makes me feel trapped."

"Well, the world is definitely falling apart around us. And it makes you not want to miss out on anything." Marabea struck up a mischievous grin. Fiarette didn't.

"But morality is supposed to comfort you. It shouldn't make you sweat it out and remind you that you're guilty of the things you find the most hateful. Make you wonder how you can be moral and still do immoral things. I'm sure I know the meaning of the word."

"Maybe you're afraid of love — it gives you the jitters because it's too respectable."

Fiarette stared. "It's just that love seems so final."

CHAPTER 16

In the fight between you and the world, back the world.

Franz Kafka

Fiarette was making dinner: The recipe said to cook the pea soup gently — gently is softer than simmer. She wanted to make it perfectly — don't let it boil, you'll make it burn. But the flame went out.

She had dreamed about an office last night, the same place she had just walked out of with everything set up differently. The word processors and the printers were facing the window instead of the wall. The clothes closet was just like the clothes closet in the back of her kindergarten classroom. Her coat was missing but there on the floor of the kindergarten closet was a pair of beat-up earth sandals she had thrown out just that morning. Everything was history but not all out of the past. Martin was in the dream; she gave him what was left of a can of soda.

She had woken up earlier than usual Sunday morning. Not working agreed with her. She felt serene if not happy. The streets echoed the voice of someone belting out the words to "Somewhere" from *West Side Story*. There was no melody, just a plea. Hold my hand and I'll take you there. What should you feel like when you're making love, she wondered. How lost should you get in the prosperity of passion? What kind of scars should you risk? The only time she had ever really floated was when she used to take acid. She smiled. Those days were over, but their accumulated forces were there. There were more and more things she had no interest in doing unless she was stoned. It made her feel the delights of the frontlines. She supposed she could have made the pea soup straight. But it always felt as though it got lots thicker if she tended to it while she was stoned. It demanded patience, making pea soup did, and getting it right was serious. She shook lots of raw garlic and cayenne pepper in it. She read in *Science Times*, "The superconductor supercollider will let physicists explore the structure of matter by colliding subatomic particles at unprecedented energies." She wished she knew more about DNA and the genetic code. She wished there was time to learn everything about the luminous gigantic landscape. But she had learned that prayers don't work if you start asking for too many things.

She could feel a mix of sympathy and resentment stirring in her and wondered why she had exchanged phone numbers with Marabea at Bagel Buffet. At first she had felt such disinterest. She hadn't even wanted to acknowledge the girl's presence at the table and then next thing she was giving her the telephone number. There was something about that girl that begged attention, if not protection. Fiarette knew her reaction to the girl was not charitable, but she didn't feel like being nice.

In the laundermat that morning an old man who was getting over a chest cold and a girl with long brown hair, originally from Pennsylvania, were talking about how the dryer time had changed from nine minutes to seven minutes so you had to put your second quarter in sooner. The conversation started when the girl noted that the washers had gone up from four quarters to six. Fiarette listened, added nothing, and watched her machine; it was stuck in rinse cycle number one; Sue, the Chinese lady who ran the place, told her it was a "slow" machine and just be patient. Twenty minutes later it was still in rinse cycle number one and Sue pulled the plug out. She was so short she had to climb on a chair and then on the washing machine to get behind it to pull the plug.

Back in her apartment sorting the laundry on her bed, she

thought about Martin. She was addicted to romance; she liked beginnings. Exciting and mysterious as they were, though, the more beginnings you gloried in, the more endings you had to endure. She knew that romance brought with it imbalance; sooner or later you get lonely, but you want to be alone.

She considered telling Martin that he was hurting her by the sin of omission. But what sin was that exactly; precisely what was he leaving out? Was it even something he was capable of giving? What was he not doing? Martin was such a good guy. The meanest thing he had ever done was try to convince her that word processing builds character, "like trigonometry," he had added, with a chuckle. But he was dead serious when he added, "I'm not trying to make you feel bad; I'm just trying to educate you. Unfortunately, griping is what you like."

Her telephone rang.

Marabea had dialed Fiarette's number. She didn't know where the temptation came from. She wasn't even thinking of her. She thought she was thinking of making pasta. The sauce, chunky style with extra tomatoes and peppers, was 70 calories a serving or 210 calories for the whole jar. The entire pound of pasta was 1600 calories, so she figured even if she ate the whole pound, which she wasn't planning to do but which could happen, it would be 2,000 calories. It was a lot of calories but she had eaten more. Then she wondered what Fiarette was doing. She imagined her voice, dusty and sad. She dialed the number and realized she didn't want to speak, but to listen. "Hello," Fiarette's voice answered, just as she had imagined it. "Hello?" Marabea hung up quietly while Fiarette was still on the line. She finished making the pasta and ate one big dish, about a third of the pound, and didn't know what to do with herself. She dialed Fiarette's number again. This time the voice was angry. "Who is this?" Marabea wondered how mad

Fiarette would let herself get. She wondered if she would start cursing. She wondered what kind of curse words she liked. She wondered if she might even suspect somebody specific, not Marabea of course, but maybe Fiarette would drop a name and give Marabea a clue about her life. But Fiarette slammed the phone down.

The next time they met, Marabea, sounding appalled, said, "I've been getting these weird phone calls lately. Somebody calls up and they don't say a thing; they don't even breathe hard, they just listen and hang up."

"My God, me, too," Fiarette said. "I can't imagine who it is."

"You, too? I wonder if it's somebody we both know."

"But who do we both know?"

Marabea wished they had something to share. She wanted to move in closer. She felt the same despair she had felt that morning when she had to clean an apartment downtown near Battery Park, a spacious apartment with not much in it. It was always a treat to clean an apartment that wasn't that dirty to begin with, but it hardly ever happened. Most people were such pigs. She was sure it was because they were so helpless they never stopped moving. When she walked in with her cleaning supplies, a tape was on. Someone who sounded like Linda Ronstadt was singing a song where all you could hear was "by my side." The girl who lived there wore a white baseball cap from a poker tournament and was having her breakfast: a small bowl of cereal and poland spring water with lots of ice. Marabea was sure everyone who met this perky creature wished they could be her best friend, even for an afternoon. She cleaned around her, feeling the glaring boundary between them. When Marabea emptied the wicker wastebasket, she saw a price tag for a bra that had cost $48 and wondered what it would be like to think you were worth a forty-eight dollar bra. Marabea hated her. She decided that when she got the chance she would graffiti her name and phone number in the subway someplace and write something dirty.

Talking to Fiarette now reminded Marabea of the anxiety from that morning. She wanted to have something these girls wanted. She wanted them both to want to be her friend.

Fiarette picked that moment to say, "I probably won't be seeing you around any more." She was so casual about it. Marabea was unnerved. Her head turned, "What do you mean?"

"I'll be up in the country all summer."

"What country?"

Fiarette laughed. "The Catskills. My boyfriend rented a house for us."

"Martin?"

"How'd you know his name?" She was surprised. "I'm sure I never called him by his name."

"Yes you did."

Marabea let the hot coffee burn her lips. "Are you going away for the whole summer?"

"Yeah. I'm not working any more anyway so it's perfect."

"You're lucky. I bet things always seem to fall right into your lap."

"That isn't true, believe me."

"Do you think I'm neurotic?" Marabea's eyes were downcast.

"I don't know you well enough to answer that."

Marabea wished Fiarette had added the word "yet" like "I don't know you well enough *yet* to answer that question."

"Who knows what neurotic means," Fiarette said.

Silence.

Rocking back and forth, Marabea said, "You seem to be excellent in everything."

"You don't even know me; do you really think of me like

that?"

"You have no idea." Fiarette felt uneasy. Marabea was dead serious. "It's romantic."

"What's romantic?"

"Your life. What you tell me about it."

Fiarette wondered what she had told her about it.

"There is nothing romantic about being with the wrong man."

"How do you know he's the wrong man?"

"I don't know if he's the wrong man or if he's just not the right one." She laughed. "Oh, Marabea, don't take it so seriously. He's just not a romantic man; he doesn't even think imperfect thoughts. He's too organized. Everything he does has a beginning and an end."

"Maybe he'll be more disorganized in the country."

"That's a nice thought. I hope so, but I'm beginning to think he likes to live by pattern and design."

Fiarette noticed how dark her face looked, "What are you so unhappy about?"

"I'm unhappy about not being beautiful." She sat at the booth with her legs apart, her elbows on the table and her palms under her chin. Her fat face looked squished.

"What's so important about beauty. You are what you are."

"Things are never important to the people who have them. Anyway, you're unhappy and I'm unhappy. That makes us equal."

Silence.

"I had a boyfriend a couple of years ago. He used to make a big thing about whose drink cost the extra dollar. I began to see there was no way he would ever treat me even to a can of coke and it started really hurting. One time we went to a movie and we got out and it was pouring rain. He hailed a cab and got in and didn't even offer to drop me off. I bet no one would ever do something like that to you."

CHAPTER 17

No one ever lacks a good reason for committing suicide.

Caesar Pavese

Theresa had never been able to picture herself this alone, this afraid of thunder and lightning. The storm had been awful; it blew the room up with light. Her kitten with the one eye didn't make a nervous move, just rubbed closer to her. She began to understand loneliness as never before. She believed it was inevitable. She saw that it was part of the human condition. She had never imagined loneliness would come like this, with her husband dying first. Death diminishes scope and afterwards nothing is the same. She felt that the flow of her life had never been a flow at all, but a jolt. Even her memories, their details and descriptions, had become a jolt. She was never prepared for life's classical motion: the unexpected. Even a friend who surprised her by showing up uninvited for morning coffee upset her balance. But death, vague and insulting, had left her fatigued. She worked with small stabs of reason, feeding the monster and trying to stop making sense of someone dying so suddenly just like that; but she made no progress. She was not enthusiastic about being reasonable; she was not sure it worked. The rest of the world, the so-called rational rest of the world, the world she knew she should be more of a part of, seemed so dissatisfied, always justifying equations. Love inspired fear. She raised a glass of red wine and prayed, "God, I want everything back in place." She drained it.

Some bird seals came in the mail from a nature foundation and she decided she would stick them on the envelopes when she paid her mortgage and the gas and telephone bills. Some of the birds looked like flowers. She loved the seals that came through the mail from the Sierra Club and the Easter Seal Foundation and the American Lung Association and always paid for them.

Very late that night she stood by the window. In the second story window of the white clapboard colonial across the street she thought she was seeing things. There was a body in the window. She thought it was a joke. There was a bag over the head — it looked like a brown paper grocery bag — and jungle green baggy pants on the body. A dog was whining in the street. Ten minutes later she looked again and it was still there. A white ceiling light was overhead and a yellow light came from somewhere behind the body. She was sure it was a joke. No one would hang himself in the window just like that.

Early the next morning it was raining even though the weatherman had said it wouldn't. She looked again; it was perfectly clear. The lights in the room had been on overnight. There was a flower pot on the window ledge that hadn't shown up in last night's darkness and a crack in the window pane was covered on the inside by a neatly sliced piece of cardboard. And hanging in the window was the body. She couldn't see the feet; they extended below the windowsill. She wondered if he was wearing shoes.

The boy who had committed suicide had been no older than Andy. On the evening news his mother said he was apparently distraught over a fight with his brother over a Nintendo video game. In the scuffle his brother had smashed his new Fossil watch and he stormed into his bedroom and barricaded himself there. That was all anybody knew.

It made her realize how worried she was about Andy. She would have liked to keep the entire incident from him — she would have liked to make sure he never heard the word "suicide" — but it was in all the papers.

The last time she had asked Andy about Krista, that girl he had been seeing, he had said it was over and he was "looking for a girl who doesn't blab." Most subjects she wouldn't even approach with Andy, like Spence's death. She couldn't tell if Andy cared. At the funeral home someone had used the word "perish" and later when he and Theresa were alone he told her that was no word to use for someone who had died — "it makes it sound like we evaporate."

The next week Andy traded his '83 Camaro for a '73 Porsche and even though it needed a nine hundred dollar engine job, he was pretty happy with it. Even if it didn't run he was pretty happy with it. Even if it never ran he would be pretty happy with it. It was a Porsche.

He and his friend sat on the steps and talked about the suicide.

"Freaky," he began, "it's like something that happens in the 'M' states."

"What are the 'm' states?"

"Krista used to say that — she called them the 'M' states — those obscure states in the midwest where people in the middle of the map go berserk and shoot down a whole family in five seconds."

"Like Indiana."

"Yeah, I guess, like Indiana."

"I was in Indiana once; the oil refineries there reach all the way into Chicago and the only thing of interest is the Indianapolis 500 and a theme park no one ever goes to."

"That guy across the street was nuts," Andy said. "All he ever talked about was Metallica and when he wasn't talking about them he was listening to them on his Walkman. Think about it. Did you ever see that guy without headphones? He told me a story once about how his best friend was shot in the stomach by his brother. He didn't even seem that upset about it, but he said he stayed home from school because he was shaken up. Then he told me that his brother had robbed the rent money. His mother had taken too much medicine and passed out and the money was near her pillow so his brother just took it. Didn't even do it in the house — he cut the screen to make it look like an outside job, like a real robber would, even though he lived there. Weird family."

"Yeah."

"Yeah," Andy said, "really."

"You know what someone told me yesterday? If you take three numbers all the same and divide by the sum of the three numbers, the answer will always be 37. Look." Andy's friend pulled a calculator out of his pocket and punched out 555 divided by 15 and the answer was 37; 111 divided by 3 was 37; 666 divided by 18 was 37.

"That's pretty neat."

Theresa was too tired again to peel the carrots. She kept wanting to put them in a salad but day after day she watched them rot. She stood near the kitchen window. Andy and his friend were out on the porch steps. She could hear them talking.

"Ever wonder how awesome it would be to hang with Eddie van Halen?"

"Greatness, that's what he's thinking about," Martin would tell Theresa when she relayed the overheard fascination with Eddie van Halen. "He's at the age where he's amazed by greatness. He hasn't caught up with us yet, Theresa; it's not his time to wonder who'll die first and where the person left behind will live. His life is going forward." He dropped his chin but held his eyes firm on her face. "We had that time. I remember it. Don't you?"

"You were happier than me," she said.

"Happier than you — now that's an interesting thought. If I was happier, it was because I didn't need other people the way you did. You know me better now. I haven't changed at all. Still don't need them unless they make me happy or stop me from being unhappy."

The next morning the subject of condom vending machines came up on one of the talk shows. It brought back memories to Theresa. She remembered the green couch in her living room and being crazy about a long lanky kid who sang in a rock 'n' roll band. He made her go down to the corner pharmacy and buy condoms; he was too shy. Condoms. She wondered if Andy used them. Did he buy the fancy kind? These days they were right out in the open, so visible, so many kinds. Did Martin use them? With that girl? Theresa wished she could have her brother all to herself. There were certain wonderful stages as children when they preferred each other to any friend. But maybe it only seemed that way looking back and the truth was that the times they were together happened by accident just because no one else was around.

CHAPTER 18

We have faith in our poison.

Rimbaud

Sunday was humid and the apartment was a mess. Fiarette's clothes hung everywhere, on the knobs of the shuttered doors to her bedroom, over the arm of her exercise bike and over the backs of the kitchen chairs. A purple bra was flung on the sofa pillows. A peach leotard hung over the bathtub.

Martin wouldn't care, though; he never expected her apartment to be tidy. And suddenly she understood. Martin's sin of omission was that he never expected anything of her. He accepted her just the way she was and indeed indulged her with his satisfaction. This angered her because she did not like to be less than perfect. That kind of acceptance was corrupt.

Martin was finishing up his writing for the day. He thought about the linking of characters, friend with friend, gripping witnesses, friend with foe, embracing rivals, partners and idle engines. He realized that some characters never got to confront other characters in his stories. As a matter of fact, he never allowed certain people to be in the same room alone together. Yet he would allow them to impact the lives of those they might never get to meet.

"Martin, are you afraid of my sexuality?" Fiarette asked him out of the blue when he got to the apartment a little later.

"Your sexuality?"

"Yes, you do think I'm sexy, don't you?"

"Yes, of course I do.

"Then, what is it? There's something about it you don't like."

Martin knew he had to come up with an answer. Denial was not it. "I don't know what you want me to do about it."

She really did not want anything more than a delicate clash, but she had started it.

"I want reassurance. I don't know why I need more of it as time goes by. You seem so uneasy talking about your past. You can describe your whole marriage in under twenty words. I want to know more. I want to see pictures. I tell you everything. I want you to know who I am. And I want to know who you are. But with you everything seems so secretive. I'm after intimacy."

"Not much of my life needs to be talked about."

"Yes it does. I like to know everything. It makes me feel better."

"Well, you ask me questions and I'll give you answers."

"It's not the same thing. I want you to tell me without my asking." She sounded serious.

"Fiarette, I will never understand you."

"You never tell me your dreams."

"I never have dreams."

"Everybody has dreams; they just don't remember them."

Fiarette was quiet and Martin was grateful it was over. Then she smiled and said, "You're so much nicer than I am."

"Why do you say that?"

"Because you like everybody."

He laughed.

"But you do." She was very valiant. "I think it's great to be able to like everybody; it's something I've never been able to do."

"Why is it great to like everybody?"

"Then more people would like you."

When she was alone she thought it out. She had been afraid Martin would ask if her feelings for him were changing. He had said, "I think the reason you ask me so often if I love you is because you're not sure you love me." But he had ended it there and had asked her nothing. She would not have been able to lie; no matter how many times Martin told her he loved her, he never made her feel he really did. It was a question of time before it was over, just because she had other things to do.

She remembered the seventies when you didn't have to know the people you got stoned with — you'd get high with anyone who came along. There was flair to it. When the hash pipe was passed around that big apartment they collected in in Stuyvesant Town, they were all one. You would fall out in front of a group of people you hadn't known yesterday and curl up happy as a cat. Everything, and there was so much, was rosy. The future was it, boundless and legitimate. So little of life had been lived compared to what was to come; it was truly imposing. The past was right there, too new to be considered yesterday. You lived with the accuracy of now.

Now Fiarette liked to get high alone.

CHAPTER NINETEEN

Lawrence of Arabia: "Certainly it hurts. The trick is not minding that it hurts."

Of his parlor trick of putting out matches with his bare fingers

They met once more, Marabea and Fiarette. It was not by accident. By now Marabea knew that most mornings Fiarette was in Bagel Buffet probably having a sesame bagel and coffee with milk no sugar.

"Will you have a telephone up there so I can call you if I decide to come up?" She saw Fiarette's quick worried expression, and added, "You sort of did invite me, unless you changed your mind." Her eyes were hard like coal.

"What about work," Fiarette jumped in, "Don't you have to work?"

"I'm pretty much my own boss."

"What do you do?" Fiarette was ready for anything.

"I clean apartments."

"Are you serious?"

"Yes, of course."

"You mean you clean *other* people's apartments?"

"Well, I get paid for it."

"Even though — it just surprises me that anyone would want to do it even for money."

Marabea laughed. "I'll come clean your apartment for you. I'm not that expensive and I really do a good job."

Fiarette smiled.

And Marabea said, "So what about it?"

"Well, we're not even there yet. I don't know what to expect. But I'll try to call you and maybe you can come up some time."

Words like "try" and "maybe" infuriated Marabea. Words like "some time." Something would surely happen on the way to some time. She had to pin Fiarette down. "Why don't you give me your address up there — I can write to you — say hello."

"I don't know it. Martin must have it. He takes care of everything."

"Can I call you tomorrow to get it?"

"Sure," Fiarette said, figuring she'd be out and miss the call. But the next day Marabea called for the address and the telephone number and Fiarette couldn't think of a good reason not to give it to her.

Marabea was delighted at getting the information and celebrated with a light lunch. 100 calorie Dannon Lite Yogurt. Cherry vanilla had become her favorite when she got tired of peach. She ate two at a time. She knew that if only she could be thin, she would be happy. Of that she had no doubts. Then she would be able to enjoy the good humor of cultural privilege that was denied her now. She would be thin and life would take on dramatic advances. Everything would be curable. People would be drawn to her and the rest would be history. It would be perfect if Fiarette was able to see her thin and she began to wonder how much weight she could lose before she visited Fiarette in the country. It had to be enough so it would be impossible not to notice the difference and she could hear Fiarette telling her how wonderful she looked.

She ate a third yogurt. Her mind raced with her mouth. She had so many things to share with Fiarette. She would tell her what it was like when she was a little girl, with a mother who managed to be right on top of her just by being in the same room. Her mother would read like a speed freak — which she was — turning the pages recklessly while Marabea waited for intimacy. But her mother was never as captivated by her daughter as by the rapid furious turning of the pages of her books. She had wanted to call her Gabriella after a heroine in a novel she had read, but her grandmother had said no, they'll only end up calling her Gabby. She was named Marilyn Beatrice, which her mother thought was another beautiful name. When she was about six, her mother punished her by setting a match to the ends of her hair which hadn't been that long to begin with. Her teacher found out about it and gave her a special assignment; she was to write down ten instances where she had become angry and ten where she got jealous. She remembered when her mother had sent flowers to herself for one of her birthdays and how she hated to eat with utensils. Whenever she could she would eat with her hands, preferably right out of a jar. "Well," she would say, "this will be gone by tonight," holding up a half-eaten jar of peanut butter.

On the day Marabea's mother planned to kill herself with an overdose of phenobarbital, her husband came home and tried to kill her, so she shot him with both hands on the pistol. Later, drunk on beer, wandering outside her apartment, she was pushed down the stairs by the super who told everyone he found her that way by the elevators. The whole story never came out. But Marabea didn't care. For her, family stories were a disturbance, an unfocused interference. They were stories.

She wondered what Fiarette's mother was like and if they looked alike. Did they look like mother and daughter or like two sisters? It was while she was wondering if Fiarette's mother was thin that she heard it, one of those spots that are repeated throughout the day on news radio. She heard it once and then it was rebroadcast the next twenty-three minutes and every twenty-three minutes until the late evening hours. A man was barricaded inside the Florida State Capital Building and demanded Japanese beer, Chinese food, marijuana and six hundred jelly donuts. He surrendered later that afternoon just before a story about an increase in the sales tax.

The image stayed with Marabea all day.

The next morning she started the day with a diet club meeting. She was trying to go to as many meetings as she could, because she knew she needed to hear over and over again how important it was to have a plan every day, to do something useful every day, and to remember that food was a way to postpone doing other things. Her meetings were her real world with outpourings from people who said their father was a genius and their mother had a brain the size of a pea. All you have to do is surround yourself with a few people who really love you, someone would say. Marabea would sit there wishing everyone in the room could be in an accident, something like a five-car pile-up or a head-on collision on an expressway with ten-foot flames. She especially hated the girl who spent fifteen minutes talking about how her trouble had started during the second oedipal phase between thirteen and seventeen. People were always snatching incidents out of their lives to go gunning after.

She hated when there were too many skinny people at the meetings. Skinny people who said things like "I feel weird about my food." There was one guy who was gay and wanted to talk to a rabbi about it. "But," he told everybody, "I already know what a rabbi will say; an orthodox rabbi will say homosexuality is an abomination; a conservative rabbi will say he can live with it; and a reform rabbi will say that's fine, God loves you just the way you are." Someone else said her mother never allowed her to have a thought of her own. They used expressions like "living in the solution." People always wanted to share what they did on their birthdays; all the stories were sad. The group leader tonight had said overeating has something to do with pain. A low tolerance level. Marabea felt life was too demanding. She became horrified by the amount of pain she was witness to at the meetings; exciting women in black net stockings saying they wished they were dead; people who would cry because they were hard core atheists and their roommates were moving out. She listened to sugar addicts who forced themselves to throw up after every meal, people whose jobs were their egos; people who were crushed by grief. One girl cried because she had been going to meetings for twelve years and was still fat. Someone else offered that eating, not overeating, helps you to be part of life. For a change Marabea felt inspired to talk, but when she raised her hand she was told the meeting was about to end and be sure to raise her hand next time. That woman Theresa had taken a lot of time talking again.

On her way home, she was seized by the desperateness in people and her own deficiencies were highlighted. She could feel herself wanting to eat out of exasperation, the hunger coming on suddenly, springing out of a miserable calmness. She tried to connect it so it made some sense, but she only got angrier. She was trying not to carry a dollar more than she needed so she wouldn't be tempted to eat. But that day she got so angry she cashed in a subway token and went to the health food store. She went to the popcorn counter and in the popper were a few pieces of popped corn. A few final kernels were flying out of the popper, slow to come; finally the popping stopped. "One bag of popcorn," Marabea said to the girl, handing over the dollar. The girl stared at her and said in a mean voice. "Do you see any popcorn there?" Marabea felt her face flush; the girl stared at her until Marabea stepped away and walked out, feeling terrible. She went into the candy store and took home two large Butterfingers bars.

She curled up on her sofa and watched Fred and Ginger. Fred was singing to Ginger. "There may be trouble ahead. But while there's moonlight and music and love and romance, let's face the music and dance." Marabea watched Ginger surrender to Fred's wisdom. She wondered what it would be like to be a woman who a man begs to love him. Fred and Ginger were moving faster and faster, their steps exotic, erotic, no longer damp or reluctant. The light from the lofty window in back of them was shining through Ginger's dress and lit her up. As soon as their lips met, the scene was cut. This was 1936. Marabea went to bed that night believing there was a heaven but not that many people get to go.

CHAPTER TWENTY

From an *Esquire* Magazine poll of 1,001 American
men: Would you rather read a good novel
or get a peek inside a well-built woman's blouse?

Read a novel: 46.5% /Get a peek: 52.7%

the last three weeks in June

The road leading up to the house was red clay and towering trees, mostly hemlocks, met in the middle. Wildflowers were everywhere. The house was pale pink stone on several gentle, sloping acres, some cleared and some in a damp forest filled with rhododendron. The house was big with wallpapered walls and painted floors and off the kitchen was a pantry with a tiny window that looked out at the forest. Upstairs was an office where Martin spent a good part of every afternoon.

"The house has a name," Kate and Teddy had told them

before setting off. "We call it 'Ezgadi' — that's the angel who helps with the successful completion of journeys." Fiarette's eyes had widened.

Outside, corners of solitude were everywhere. She wandered and climbed and made discoveries every day — a dark green wicker chair with a stone for a leg under an apple tree circled by a stone wall, a grape arbor beyond the house where a gray bench sat under an oak at a clearing in the woods, the top floor of the barn where she gazed out a window and studied the sky on the pasture or the weathered deck covered by bayberry and juniper.   She was struck by the beauty of the greens of the trees. Again she was jubilant; life was splendid. And then there was the pond.

"Here's the best surprise," Martin said their first day there.

"Where?"

"Come with me."

He led her away from the house, toward a semicircle of forsythia, through it and into the arm of a huge hemlock, its branches obscuring a narrow stone path carved out of high grasses. It was perfectly camouflaged and Fiarette thought she was walking right into a tree. They had to walk single file for a couple of hundred feet and there it was, a pond that looked as big as an acre with a bank of clover and buttercups. Weatherbeaten Adirondack chairs and an old wood table painted white stood around it.

"This is amazing," Fiarette said.

"Yes, I'll finally be able to swim all I want," Martin said. "I hope you brought a bathing suit."

The next morning they went to a rummage sale at a Methodist church over a covered bridge. Fiarette bought some hand-decorated tea towels, four for a dollar, with a pink and green art deco design on them. And then they drove to Tyler Hill and had a big breakfast of English muffins and cheese and ham.

★★★

A few days later Martin found a letter for Fiarette in the mailbox down by the road. Fiarette was at the kitchen table eating cheerios and bananas when he handed it to her. She saw it was from Marabea and read the whole thing but not so she'd remember. "I'm sure you have other friends with whom you have more in common than you do with me," Marabea had written. "I know friends come and go and new friends take their place." Fiarette couldn't understand it; did this girl really think whatever it was they shared was friendship? Did she really think it had any promise of continuing? Was this girl Marabea so lonely she was able to talk herself into a bond with someone she hardly knew? Women always did this with men, but Fiarette wondered why they would do it with each other. Friendship, she decided, can be just as compelling as a love affair.

"I think, quite simply, we live in two different worlds," Marabea had written. "It is that simple," was the next line. By the next day Fiarette had forgotten about the letter.

At a garage sale she bought a satin pillow cover with a map of Atlantic City when the steel pier was still there and a small oil painting of apples in a basket that she hung in the bathroom. She was able to make pea soup and not burn it. She picked flowers and tomatoes and found a hand-tied quilt at a yard sale for eight dollars.

One night they went to a penny social at the firehouse, where an American flag was flying at each end of the long room. It was the kind of social everyone could afford, a night out that could cost as little as a dollar. A dollar a person entitled you to two things: a refreshment (coffee, always exceptionally good, or punch, plus your choice of a piece of cake and cookie or a piece of cake and a brownie or two chocolate cup cakes, all home made); and a card with 25 perforated numbers, all the same, which you deposited one by one in paper cups from Burger King that were scotch-taped to prizes beside them.

The empty cups and the prizes were arranged on long wooden tables. You would deposit as many perforated numbers as the number of chances you wanted to take on an item, things like a bag of potato chips, coat-hangers, a pot of violets, refried beans, bubble bath or a pillow that said BETH.

At seven things got underway. "On behalf of the ladies guild of St. Francis Church, I want to thank everyone for coming tonight. I hope everyone is a winner. Please keep your hand up until you receive your prize so the runners don't lose you. If you have small children, please watch them so they don't get trampled by the runners." Local kids got to be runners and deliver the prizes.

When the actual calling begins, the room is hushed. Most of the numbers called started with 52's and 63's so Fiarette didn't have to pay that close attention, which was fine with her, because all her numbers began with 79: 7968 - 7969 - 7982 - 7987. She was trying to catch the eye of a guy in a black T-shirt sitting a few rows in front of them. He had black hair and a chiseled face. The one she thinks is his wife sat on his left and, from the back, looked like she had bad posture. Now he was talking to the woman on his right, his profile as striking as he was head on; she wore a faded red T-shirt and looked like a farmer. Fiarette hoped neither one was his wife. Martin sat quietly next to her drinking coffee watching his numbers. The woman behind them won a package of Cheer and a Food Club fudge brownie mix. The guy with the black shirt got up and Fiarette noticed he limped. Now she could read the back of his shirt: it said Interstate Motor Plaza. She found the limp sexy.

The man next to her had already won twice — a can of chunk light tuna and a package of cocktail napkins — when one of Fiarette's numbers was called and she came home with three Avon guest soaps.

★★★

They started going to auctions. There was the weekly favorite: 5:30 Thursday night at the barn where the auctioneer was the justice of the peace. They would leave the house early and be one of the first there, becoming themselves familiar faces, like the man who wore a light blue cotton hat to keep the setting sun out of his eyes and a tie clip with the head of a horse. He came with his father and scrutinized everything, taking tiny objects in his hands and turning them over mindfully, but never bidding. One girl was just back from picking tobacco in West Virginia; last week she took home a purple flowered bedspread and an electric mixer. There was an antique dealer, big-boned and solemn-faced. A more serious auction was held on Saturday nights where you were handed the Terms of Sale when you walked in. "If a dispute arises between two or more bidders, the decision of the auctioneer shall be final and absolute." Auctions like that had drop-sided oak tea trolleys and polished pine dressing tables.

Whenever something good came up at auction, the auctioneers all used the same line. "This'll make you change your tune." Fiarette found things she wanted, but nothing she wanted that much. The fun was in bidding, winning the bid, taking it home and unwrapping it. After that, it had limited appeal, except for the big plaster collie she used as a doorstop to the dining room.

They would go on long drives, heading west until they stopped seeing people, just trees, telephone poles, broken yellow lines and an occasional sign that such and such was the oldest house in the village. The roads became main streets and then roads and then main streets. American flags were flying everywhere. Most houses were white. Lots of brown cows. Tom-Cat archery. Summer shadows. Dragon City Chinese restaurant, Get one while it's hot, an ad for Kawasaki, another flag on a front porch. Road Crews, red tractors, junction signs, yellow on blue, pots of geraniums on stone posts. They drove past the Lakeview Luncheonette; a green and red tin sign outside was painted with an ice cream cone; the "L" in Lakeview was written one way and the "L" in Luncheonette was written in a different script even though both were capital letters. The land stopped climbing and began to roll; there were signs for sweetcorn. Everything was so beautiful it was scary. Slowly the city began to lose its attraction; it felt threatening.

She found a stack of Organic Gardening magazines and loved the names of the vegetables: royal burgundy snap beans, lady bell peppers, lemon boy tomatoes, gold rush zucchini. She looked at the ad for strawberry plants. "One berry makes a mouthful. Three berries fill both hands." What would it be like to grow strawberries, to sip freshly brewed coffee and to read letters to the editor of a country newspaper? "Last spring I wrote to you about the poor germination of my sugar snap peas. You said to plant the seed one half to three-quarters inch deep, not as deep as the seed package recommended."

Could her environment persuade her what to be? Could being one hundred miles away from New York make her so different? Was a spiritual landscape all she needed? Would this be the place where she might fit in all of the time?

Some nights they took long walks just before dark, down their road past a big barn with white curtains, an old hotel and a little white schoolhouse at the corner. "Isn't it funny," she said to Martin, "how practical life feels up here?" He smiled without a word; he knew exactly what she meant.

She was sorry she had left her journal at home and started pasting things like pressed flowers and old penny social tickets in a thirty-nine cents composition book from the Trading Post, a general store with mostly hardware. She stopped wearing make-up and pulled her hair back. Martin told her he liked the way she looked. Maybe a new life might not be so perilous a frontier after all.

But at the Saturday night auction the only thing Fiarette was interested in was the boy carrying merchandise out from the back rooms and holding it up for bid. She had seen enough depression glass and old copies of *Life* to last a lifetime. He was thin with as much torso as legs and a smile that stayed on his face; he wore thick glasses, so thick she could hardly see the color of his eyes. She wanted desperately to talk to him. She knew just how she would handle it, just how to proceed, a master at conquest. Abruptly, again, Martin didn't seem right. She couldn't say a bad word about him and she knew she was the villain. It wasn't anybody's fault. It was just the way it was.

One Sunday they decided to go to mass at a little country church. Everyone sang "Let there be peace on earth and let it begin with me." At the end of mass, the priest addressed some June graduates, the boys in red gowns, the girls in white. He told them about an acrobat, who we love because he flies through the air on his own momentum, flies, takes the risk of reaching the "unsupported moment." He urged them to go forward, to fly through the air, and return, heroes and heroines.

CHAPTER 21

We don't make mistakes here
We just learn great lessons.

From Hawaii Five-O

Marabea didn't know what she was doing on the bus. All she knew was that Shortline went up to the Catskills and that was where she wanted to be. It hardly mattered where and it didn't matter how. She just wanted to be there as quickly as possible. She was seized by a frenzy that was as lucid as they come and pushed her closer to the unnamed. She had no way of knowing how close the bus would come to where she wanted to be but being on that bus made her feel better. She wanted to be near where Fiarette was to breathe the same air.

It was two hours before the first stop, the Monticello bus station. The ride up filled her with her own imbalances, a willful but useless urging.

The bus pulled in and emptied. Four people got off: a fat woman with a red football shirt, a Chinese man with two plastic bags, a young boy in blue shorts and Marabea. She went straight to the candy machine.

Willy would never have believed it would be so easy to get out. While a dozen other inmates were in the recreation yard he escaped by climbing an eighteen-foot fence and sliding between the fence and the roof. It was as good as an open door.

He walked out of the beige building with barbed wire, away from the sign that said "Sullivan County Jail" with black arrows pointing towards the visitors' entrance. Three more stairs down, kids hung around throwing a ball against the beige brick wall. A black woman sat on the hood of a red car, like a Christmas ornament. He passed the sign "Communications with prisoners prohibited; Visitors will be prosecuted." He walked out and took a smile with him. He crossed North Street and turned back only once to see a white frame house across from the jail and the sign Sheriff's Patrol Headquarters. He looked at the screens and bars and wood slats on the upper buildings. Down North Street and over to Broadway, past the Matthew Bible Institute, the free municipal parking, past a bar called Wild Thing, past Catskill Laundry and senior housing and the Elks Club where there was bingo every Tuesday night at 7:30. Past the Ambulance Corps. to the bus terminal, a simple concrete block building with a few benches outside. There was one bus there, a local bus. A guy wearing a plastic jacket, his face flat with vacant eyes, cuddled a small valise in his lap; it was brown with cream stripes. He opened it and took out a can of Schaefer. He had red hair and was with a girl who chewed bubble gum and blew loud noisy bubbles.

Willy listened to the motors of the buses; now there were four, two local, one going north and the last going to New York City.

He never saw her there throwing a wrapper into the green wastebasket. A candy bar wrapper. She was still chewing. She took her wristwatch off and held it up to her ear and shook it as though time had stopped. She walked over to the wastebasket and threw another wrapper away. Corn chips, funny bones and Plantation brownies. Marabea had a pocketful of goodies.

Everyone was a loser. The black woman with the purple shirt and bored look. The Pointer Sisters sang "I'm so Excited" over the radio. Everyone was either alone or with children. Looking down at their feet. Kids eating M & M's, a girl with permed hair, her feet tapping, a man in a gray jacket, legs crossed and foot shaking. A big plant growing towards the recessed ceiling lights.

Willy sat on a plastic seat facing the ticket booth where a girl selling tickets wore her hair in a pony tail. The room was all windows but he never saw Marabea. "Now boarding Bus 294 to New York City." Marabea got on. The only upstate air she got to breathe was the fumes at the bus station.

Willy sat there facing the wall and picked up a newspaper and saw this ad: "Happy Jack Mange Lotion, promotes healing and hair growth to any mange, hot spot, fungus on dogs and horses. At better farm feed and hardware stores."

He watched the intercounty buses, slow moving and not many of them. They all stopped in Monticello where people got off to go someplace else. He thought about taking a local bus and going to see his wife, back to the gray trailer with the bird house outside, across from the auto wreck place with old yellow school buses that sat in overgrown weeds. His wife used hub caps to keep the oilcloth tablecloth outside from blowing away. Back to where he had come from, back to the life where all people had to wait for was the weather to change. Here comes the sun, they might say. Followed by, whoops, it's gone again.

But his wife would find something to blame him for and he wasn't sure he ever wanted to see his family again. His four year old was a poignant child who lined up blocks and didn't do much else, no conversation, no eye contact, focused on a single thing, usually something mechanical. He had no understanding of time and reversed pronouns and never understood the difference between me and you. You would use you when speaking to him and he didn't understand if he was you. He was affectionate, but couldn't come to terms, never waved goodbye and would never understand how to start a conversation.

★ ★ ★

The local headlines shouted "Murder Suspect Slips Past Police Four Times". What that really meant was that Willy had been arrested four times for minor crimes and computer checks turned up nothing. It wasn't until his escape that police found he was wanted for stabbing a girlfriend to death four years ago. "Very often we find these people in local jails after they've been arrested for other crimes," a Manhattan detective said. Police were unable to explain how Willy's previous criminal history never seemed to catch up with him. The papers reported that in the first three days police racked up 720 hours in overtime or $18,000 in extra pay. Helicopters flew overhead and dogs patrolled. There were unconfirmed sightings but nothing turned up. Correction union officials called for a second razor wire fence around H block, where Willy had been housed. "The positive appearance may have led some to forget the purpose and mission of a jail," a member of the correction advisory board said. He wanted a perimeter fence and a checkpoint.

Willy Saunders had no world. It continued to revolve far beyond him. The headlines belonged to somebody else. Life was a network of sidelines. Fishing and hunting licenses were about to expire. The sports section said Blackhawks Force Oilers into 3-0 Hole. Prices dropped on the Fed's inaction. The media talked about single motherhood, Honda dealers and the urging of the mayor to cease violence all in the same breath. An old lady complained to the police that the man across the street was mowing the grass in his underwear. The best song around was Bonnie Raitt's "Let's give them something to talk about." Love was waiting to happen.

He decided to drift.

CHAPTER 22

**I was looking for a lifestyle
that did not require my presence.**

Kinky Friedman

Sometimes Andy was in the mood to listen to songs with names like "Jacking for Beats" and "I Wanna Sex You Up". But not always. He was trying to understand potential and lived with restructured loyalties and blurry allegiances. He worried that he would always feel like things had to be reshuffled, that collision would become part of his consciousness. He was learning about sex, that it wasn't always inspiring. The music went too fast and the best part turned out to be thinking about it before it happened. He wished he had something to obsess about. Answers were there, but not the ones he wanted. He wanted things to be easier and he was fearful of a damaged ego. He wished he could meet a girl he loved enough to go off and live in a tent with. Short of that, everything had deficits.

He would wake up, unsure of his mood until things started to happen and the day peeled away. At its worst it could be a ruthless day where everything hurt. But he would get through it and no one would know his real feelings. Sometimes you got a clue from the message he left on his answering machine which was usually just loud music followed by the click of the telephone receiver. Other times he would sound very enterprising. And sometimes he didn't turn the machine on at all.

In the morning's mail was a letter from his Uncle Martin, a handwritten note. "I just want you to know I'm thinking about you. Why don't you come up to the country and see me?"

When Martin had written that note, he had wanted to put "and see me and my girl." It sounded more honest. But the emotion he felt for Andy was too private to sign somebody else's name to. He wanted Andy to understand how much love was available to him from an uncle, someone right there, someone not that different from him after all. It had started out a much longer letter, had gone through a couple of drafts and in its final stage was scribbled haphazardly on a sheet of plain paper to make it look like it had just come off the top of his head. He had put something in there telling Andy to love himself and to resist the temptation to give in to greed of any kind. But he took it out. He had tried to explain the difference between exciting and frivolous, but he took that out, too.

Martin wanted to know if Andy missed Spence, and who Spence had been to him.

But Andy didn't think too much about Spence at all, remembering him as a man who couldn't be in a room without a radio on. It didn't have to be blasting. It was noise, distant and steady. And when the subject of money came up Spence would always say, "I tell you, it doesn't mean a thing." Andy was unsure what he meant by that and didn't know whether to like him or dislike him for it.

He spent a lot of time trying to figure his mother out. He saw her cry sometimes and wondered if it was because she missed Spence or whether it was something else. But he knew he had never seen her cry when Spence had been alive.

Theresa reminisced about Spence; she remembered the first night they had gone out. She hadn't seen him for four months, and the last time had been at his wife's funeral. They had decided to have dinner and she waited in her car in the parking lot for him. She wondered what color car he would have. He had told her that his mechanic said his old car, a 1978 Dodge, had 214,000 miles on it and it was time for a new one.

A widower; what color car would he choose? She ruled out red. It turned out to be a dazzling gray.

She remembered how irritated he used to get her. He would go to the supermarket and wrap every single vegetable in a small plastic bag of its own and then tie it with a tight knot. A lemon. A lime. Four peaches. Two cucumbers. An onion. A banana. Each one in its own tightly wrapped plastic bag. She would be cooking with greasy hands that could never untie those slippery knots and she had to tear them open with her teeth. Now she missed that. He would make fun of her panic attacks and tell her she should go live in a bubble with a lock. She missed that. Even though Andy was right there in the house, she felt she was living alone.

"Why don't you call Krista up?" Theresa said to Andy. He was growing more and more remote.

"I haven't seen her in months, Ma." He talked without looking up. He was letting his toast get cold.

Theresa wondered if he hadn't seen Krista or Krista hadn't seen him. But she knew better than to ask; romance was such a touchy issue. She was convinced romance was not worth its complicated rewards; independence was worth more. She watched Andy forget about his toast and was happy when the phone rang and her friend Rose down the street suggested lunch.

Rose was out shopping for silver napkin rings. "No more paper napkins," she said, "only cloth napkins from now on." "I want to make dining an experience," she told Theresa in the antique shop where she bought a pair of thick hallmarked sterling silver napkin rings for one hundred dollars each.

Later, they stopped at the Oakwood Café where they both had mushroom barley soup and tuna on pumpernickel. Rose had iced tea and Theresa had her fifth or sixth mug of coffee for the day.

"Spence didn't want to die," Theresa told her. "There were too many things he enjoyed — cherished."

Rose talked about her daughter who had put in an application for a cashier's job at the supermarket, but the application was lost and someone else was given the job.

Rose was just getting ready to talk about her son David who was in analysis and thinking of being a dentist when Theresa said "I started to study The Lord's Prayer. I wanted to understand what made it so special. I decided the most important part is the words 'thy will be done.' I ought to get my brother to explain those words to me. He's always talking about resigning your will to the will of God."

"How is your brother?"

"Going out with someone who doesn't appreciate him." Her answer was clipped while she studied the menu for the gooiest dessert. "You know, my eyesight gets worse every day."

Rose nodded her head in understanding. "Everything gets worse. My sister-in-law had a face lift last year. She's only forty-two. It cost seven thousand dollars. When I went to pick her up she looked absolutely awful but every week she got prettier and prettier and people started asking her if she was in love or something she looked so terrific." Rose's eyes began to shine.

Theresa wondered if her brother wanted his girlfriend's youth for his own.

Rose was still talking about her sister-in-law. "Her therapist told her she should think about other things besides losing her looks. He told her men don't always need the most beautiful woman on their arms. And I keep getting permanents because I don't know what to do with my hair."

They sipped their coffee in silence, until Theresa said "Spence was always telling me I had no goals. I told him goals are for kids, not women my age. What am I supposed to want?"

On Sunday Theresa went to the nine o'clock mass. Father Steven gave her a broken Holy Communion host and she was wondering if he was going to give her the other half of the broken piece or whether she should walk away from the altar. She folded her hands in prayer and walked back to her seat. The communion hymn was "Amazing Grace" but the closing hymn was something Theresa had never heard and no one seemed to know. The organist played with only two or three voices going. I love God but I am getting less holy, she was thinking.

Theresa felt the panic of being alone. She would never be able to think she had "all the time in the world" — who could dare think it? She had trouble sleeping, sweating even under a single cotton sheet. She tossed and turned and wondered why. She put her hand between her legs looking for memorized passion and pulled it away. Her own body disgusted her, left her sour. She would get up from bed and turn on the night table light and look around the room. Nothing ever changed. She was the only one who could change it but she was too tired. Her new prayer became "Let Jesus Take Over."

The next morning Andy and Theresa bumped into each other in the kitchen. "I'm going to see Uncle Martin, Mom. He wrote me a letter asking me to come visit him."

"Why can't he ever pick up a telephone? Why does he have to write letters even though we all live in the same city?"

"He's not *in* the city; he's in the country."

"Even when he's in the city, he writes."

"He's a writer, Mom," Andy said with some reverence.

"How long are you going to stay? Are you sure there's enough room?"

"I'm going up for the holiday. I'll take a bus up Thursday

and he'll pick me up."

"He didn't say anything about me coming?"

"No, Ma." Her name had not even come up.

"He's up there with that girl."

The Fourth of July was on a Thursday which meant no work on Friday and a four-day weekend.

Marabea felt threatened by long weekends. All everybody talked about was picnics and having a good time. After her diet club meeting she had fallen into a deep sleep. She woke up not knowing if it was morning or night. An expression from her diet club meeting came back to her — "morbid dependency." She was frightened by the shrewdness of an addiction, to chocolate, to pills, to scraping at invention to make life more reasonable.

She was tired of going to meetings where the complexities of other people's lives were paralyzing her own. The designs and strategies of her beloved Hollywood films always made sense, always had hope, even the tragedies. But real life meant you were entrenched in some contrived determination.

Morbid dependency: it had something to do with the fear of being excluded, with bonds being formed when she was not there to stake her claim. She remembered waiting for her parents to come home, being very young where her impact was more like a strain, fearful that her parents would not return, that they would find some other little girl to love and would forget her in a moment. The terror was awful and it went back so far she could not trace it. It prevailed in her and she could not tell if it was real or if she was making it up. Morbid dependency, repetition compulsion, words from far-off places, words that sounded like her. She felt crazy. She wanted to stop thinking. She got out of bed and smelled food everywhere but couldn't tell what any of it was. She didn't want Fiarette to be friends with anybody else. She couldn't think beyond that; anything else was too involved.

She flicked on cable and the shopping channel. She hoped she saw something she liked so she could use the Visa card number she had memorized when the girl whose apartment she was cleaning ordered something over the phone. The first thing offered was a pearl earring set for forty-seven dollars. Everything was sold with the promise of how well it would go with something else. The earring set quickly sold out. Next up was Twilite Tan, a lotion and scrub to make you look like you had been in the sun all day. It was being marketed under the name of Frankie Avalon's Twilite Tan. Frankie was there shaking his head yes because someone had called in to praise his product and said no one should worry about turning orange. "If you want it darker, put it on twice a day," Frankie said. The next item was the "hottest suede jacket" that came with a hunter green and jungle tan skirt, the two "hottest" suede colors. It did come in extra large but Marabea didn't want it. There was an Egyptian cartouche and another set of earrings with "71 crystals per ear."

For months Marabea had worn stretch pants, winter weight and summer weight. They stretched and grew with her. The ones they were selling on the shopping club were fancier than sweat pants. They were pleated at the waist, had ankle straps, and wide waistbands with tiny gold buttons. She ordered three pair.

But tomorrow, she decided, tomorrow she would wear her jeans even if they were too tight.

CHAPTER 23

From Friends in the Sea,
Environmental Defense Fund calendar for June

Common dolphin (delphinus delphis).
Dolphins live in large, fluid societies numbering up to
1,000 individuals. Scientific studies suggest that
dolphins do a great deal of vocalizing and touching to
maintain complex social ties.

In New York City the song of the big holiday weekend seduced everyone. Anywhere there was water there were people. They streamed there by car, by boat, by bus, by train. People who had no place to go made something up fast.

Up in the country day-long picnics were followed by patriotic speeches and fireworks. Hot dogs for parade participants would be donated and parades would go on, rain or shine, in every valley and on every mountain top. At night the Fire Department on Route 434 would have a four thousand dollar super bingo night. Just after midnight there would be fatal crashes: a subcompact would collide head-on with a mini van and traffic would be tied up with cars routed on back roads around the site of the crash. Someone else would fail to negotiate a left corner and drive off to the right into a ditch. But it was now morning and Marabea was driving west along Route 17 where the license plate on the car in front of her said The word of God is the will of God.

Around noon Fiarette sat at the kitchen table and studied the carton of milk. Dairy fresh pasteurized homogenized milk with two reindeer facing each other. She was sure they were reindeer, outlines of white against red, because they didn't look like cows. She wondered what reindeer were doing on a carton of milk. The sound of a car coming up the long driveway snapped Fiarette out of her daydreams. The car stopped short. Marabea had arrived. She stepped out wearing jeans that were so tight she couldn't have put a stick of gum in her pockets. She strolled past Fiarette into the kitchen while Fiarette stood stunned at the half-open screen door.

"What are you doing here?" Fiarette said in a very excited voice. "You should have called."

"I rented it." Marabea waved grandly at the white Toyota, peered over the tops of her purple rimmed sunglasses and answered Fiarette. "I didn't want you to go to any trouble."

Martin walked through the room with an open book in his hand. *Raising Milk Goats the Modern Way*.

"What are you reading that for?" Fiarette screeched, like a mad woman.

"Because it's interesting." He tightened his face. "What's wrong with you — you're in a rotten mood."

Fiarette answered by turning her head toward Marabea, who laughed and said brightly, "I think it was me — I think I surprised her."

"This is Marabea, someone from the city," Fiarette said.

"Someone from the city." Not even "a friend from the city." Marabea would remember that.

"Well, that's great," said Martin. "Fiarette needs a friend around. I'm afraid I haven't been such good company the last few days. I'll just go back upstairs to my work and see you girls later." He took a few steps and turned back. "Just call me when Andy gets here," he said to Fiarette. "Have fun," he said to both of them, this time looking at Marabea. He walked out of the kitchen and up the stairs.

"Who's Andy?" Marabea asked right away. "I didn't expect a lot of people to be here."

Fiarette didn't know how to react. "Andy is Martin's nephew," she said.

"Do you know him?"

"No. His father died and Martin thought he needed to get away from his mother for a weekend." She threw the rest of her cereal into the sink and filled the bowl with some water. "Look, why don't we just get out of the house."

"I never throw away food," Marabea said, watching her. "I wish I had your willpower."

"I have no willpower. I would just hate being fat. If you don't need it, why eat it?"

Fiarette walked out onto the deck and slammed the screen door behind her. Marabea could feel tears in her eyes. She knew Fiarette was trying to hurt her. Driving down Main Street in the village she had seen Dari Barn. She had been hoping she and Fiarette could take a ride and get ice cream sundaes with sprinkles and whipped cream and cherries. For the Fourth of July. But now she wouldn't dare suggest it.

"He's very nice," Marabea said.

"Who?" Fiarette said, wanting to be as mean as possible.

"Martin."

"Oh, Martin," she said off-handedly. "I wish . . ."

"You wish what?"

"I wish I wasn't so important to him. I want to go back to myself, the way I was before I met him. I was alone."

"You sound like you'd rather be alone."

"I guess I would. At least when I'm alone I'm not cranky." She turned to face Marabea. "I keep trying to shape this relationship instead of just waiting for it to happen. I thought I'd get what I wanted that way. But now the idea of being loved makes me feel detached. It's awful. Sometimes when he tells me he loves me, I don't feel a thing. Instead of making me think about the future, it makes me think about the past. There's always some kind of sadness going on. And that makes me want to punish him for things he had nothing to do with." She stopped, "Why am I telling you this?" There was a cry in her voice and Marabea was quiet for fear Fiarette would stop talking and she would learn no more.

Fiarette headed down the steps of the deck and they started walking in silence, into the fields, past the berry bushes.

"Do you mind being seen with a fat person?"

"You talk like you're 200 pounds."

"Close."

"Really?"

"See," said Marabea, "it does make a difference."

"Oh, it does not. It's just that 200 pounds sounds like a heavyweight boxer."

Marabea put her hands over her ears. "Stop it," she begged. "I bet you think I've never had a real boyfriend. Well, I had plenty when I was thin."

"My God, Marabea, why don't you go to a doctor?"

"I don't know where to start," Marabea said. "I need someone to answer to."

"Can't you just answer to yourself?"

"I can't work it that way."

Back in the kitchen Fiarette was making a pot of coffee. Martin walked in, "Where's your friend?"

"She's not my friend and she's upstairs taking a shower."

Martin raised his eyebrows at her and walked over to the window and peeked out and down the driveway. "I wonder why Andy's not here yet."

"What's he like?"

"Serious. If there was only some way I could tell him not to let himself be hurt so easily, how critical it is not to feel all the punches. But what would all that mean to a kid his age? How do you learn when to stop scrutinizing? I think he scrutinizes his every thought. By the way, how'd that girl know where you were up here if she's not a friend?"

"I gave her the address."

***

Marabea walked into the kitchen; her hair was still wet. She had run a comb through it but only once. Fiarette wondered if she had overheard Martin asking about her.

Outside the kitchen window a car kicked gravel. Martin, smiling, bounced out of the kitchen onto the deck. "Great, here he is." Fiarette and Marabea followed.

And there he was. Andy, lanky and courtly, lumbered out of the car with a very small navy nylon overnight bag and held them captive. He blushed when he saw all the faces looking at him. Martin walked over and threw his arm across his shoulder. "You made it."

"Lot of traffic. *Lot* of traffic." He was looking at Martin.

"Well, you can settle in for the rest of the weekend now."

They all walked into the house. It was getting chilly.

"Did you eat?" Martin asked him.

"I grabbed someone on the way. I mean something." He had been peeking at Fiarette out of the corner of his eye and was honestly embarrassed by the slip.

After coffee Fiarette pushed her chair back from the table outside on the deck and said "I guess you two have lots to talk about."

Martin smiled at Andy. "That's not such a bad idea."

"We're going upstairs and get ready for bed. Come on, Marabea."

Marabea was happy to go.

On the stairway before they even reached the second floor, Fiarette was out of control. "Did you see him? Did you see him?" She was so happy she was jumping out of her skin.

"Who?" Marabea said, with the perfect degree of puzzlement in her big eyes.

"Who! Martin's nephew! Who else? My God, is he hot! His eyes are just full of fire." Her own eyes narrowed. "You can feel it!"

"He's just a kid."

"That's no kid," Fiarette said, knowingly. "He's adorable."

"He looks like someone who's probably very full of himself."

"Oh, Marabea, you have to know what to look for in a man." Marabea glared at her. Fiarette continued with conviction. "They're all very unique, just like women. They're not all misfits and pretty cowboys."

Marabea wondered how many men Fiarette had slept with. "Well," she said, "you have Martin. How many men do you need?" Her face was somber.

Fiarette started to laugh out loud. "Look, Martin's a great human being. We get along. We're compatible. I trust him not to hurt me. He wakes up in a good mood. But when I see someone like Andy, I forget everything else."

"You're a cruel bitch, do you know that?"

"Don't take it so seriously, Marabea. It has nothing to do with you."

Downstairs Martin and Andy sat on the steps of the deck. The scents of summer filled the air.

"It's so quiet," Andy said.

"Not too quiet, though, is it?"

Andy grinned. "Is this where you do your writing?"

"It's a great place to write."

"What makes you write? Why do you do it?" He sounded interested.

"Mostly because I don't like to talk back. A writer can put words in other people's mouths. You can wipe the grins off everybody's face. You can make people angry and lonely."

"Are you angry and lonely?"

"I don't think so, Andy."

The telephone rang in the kitchen. After three rings Martin got up and went in the house to answer it. It was Theresa.

"It's your mom," he said, and handed the phone to Andy.

His mother sounded awful. "As soon as you drove off today, I started to miss you," she said. "I felt I had failed you in some way. I don't know how to entertain you."

"Ma, I don't want you to entertain me."

"I know I get nervous and excitable about things, Andy, but I'll try to calm down."

"That's okay, Ma."

"Is your uncle's girlfriend there?"

"Yeah, ma, she's really nice."

"Well, in my day they called it jail bait."

"Ma, I have to go now."

"All right then."

He walked back out to the porch fuming and sat down across from Martin. "Sometimes I think my mother's nuts."

"Well, that could very well be," Martin said, seriously distracted by the strong possibility that it was. And then he laughed out loud and was pleased to hear Andy's laugh ring along with his own. It would be so easy to say the wrong thing, to be overzealous or underzealous or lack any kind of zeal at all. Martin realized he did not know how to act and then instantly knew there must be no acting.

But Andy had set the mood.

"I was thinking about lying recently," Martin said, "how hard it is to stay honest. If you lie long enough, you may think you're victorious. But you're not really winning anything, so victory is not possible. The last time I felt victorious was on a summer day at Montauk Point. I was young enough to be learning about fear but not yet afraid of affection. I was with my father. That's all there was to it. Nothing else happened. We were just together on an exceptionally memorable day."

Martin remembered Andy's old dinosaur collection. "Whatever happened to your dinosaurs? You had some collection — plastic ones, pink ones, serious ones, ones with clothes on. You had them lined up on every windowsill in your bedroom." Andy had as many windows in his bedroom as a boy as Martin had in his whole apartment right now.

"You know why I used to like dinosaurs?"

Martin listened.

"Because the dinosaur was proof that no matter how big something was, it could always disappear."

"Discipline transcends everything — even teaches you how to disappear," Martin told him. He did not know if that would mean much to Andy, but he wanted to say it. "Builds character. That means liberation. Don't be dependent. That's discipline. It's when you really need it that you do your growing. You do your growing in times of need."

Andy's voice was low and deliberate. "I think my mother's nuts and I'm sick of my friends. My best friend is going on his first blind date Sunday. He's going with this guy whose girlfriend is Chinese. They're going to Red Lobster. That's all they talk about — girls and what to wear."

"What do you talk about?"

Andy said nothing. He sat back and stretched his legs out in front of him. Then: "I think about death a lot but I think of it as just something that takes place. Another move."

"I think that's exactly what it is."

The silence was absorbing; there was no longer any need for language. Martin refused small talk and Andy had no questions left.

Later that night Martin remembered being Andy's age. All he wanted out of life was to live in the same city where his favorite team played baseball.

When Martin walked into their bedroom, Fiarette was asleep and having a dream. She was going on a cruise with two people; one was her father. When it was time to board, she had lost them and searched the weathered piers through long lines of people, most of whose faces were turned away from her. Everyone was being handed boarding instructions and told where their cabins were. Fiarette had no ticket, no name of a ship, no proof at all that she was sailing. Finally, her father and the other person called her over; they had their own tickets and vouchers in their hands, but none for her. One of her father's tickets was round and had "Casino" stamped on it. She begged them to come with her to get her tickets because she didn't know where to go. They didn't understand what she wanted. She was angry and frightened.

The next morning Fiarette told everyone there were four flavors of yogurt, three kinds of cereal, and fruit salad, bagels and jam. Help yourselves. She sat on the deck with a mug of coffee.

"Ginger Rogers is wheelchair-bound now, did you know that?" Marabea asked, looking up from the *Star* which she had brought with her. They were alone; Martin and Andy were rummaging around in the house.

"I feel so vulnerable," Marabea said, "like a toy."

"Because of Ginger Rogers?" Fiarette asked.

"Why do you like to make fun of me?"

"Come on, take it down a notch. I'm not making fun of you."

"I'm not important enough to make fun of."

"Why don't you go get some help, Marabea?"

"I went to a therapist once. She told me I needed intimacy and distance. She confused me right away."

Andy came storming out of the kitchen onto the deck, followed by Martin.

"God, I hate confrontation," Andy said, pounding his fists into each other, his eyes shut tight. "There's always an argument going on." He slumped down in one of the Adirondack chairs that hadn't been painted in years.

Martin looked at Fiarette. "His mother called him."

"Don't tell everyone that my mother called me, Uncle Martin." He cooled down his voice. "All I want is some peace and she doesn't even know what the word means."

"Well, that can be a pretty amazing revelation, can't it, to realize what you really want is peace," Martin offered.

Andy said nothing, so Martin went on. "Peace is something you give yourself."

Fiarette could conjure up a shadowy portrayal of peace. She could talk its talk. All she needed was the opportunity. She would fill Andy's head with concepts and theories, with suggestions about validating your feelings. She would fill his eyes with hope. She would make him feel important. She would get him to put his hands on her and curl his fingers under the skinny straps of the white cotton sundress she would wear tonight, tuck those fingers under those straps and pull her closer to him, tug her to him, like a lonesome cowboy. She wouldn't tell him peace had an anchor on it.

They all sat there quietly, Marabea still reading the *Star* and Fiarette dreaming her dreams.

"Let's take a ride over to Walnut Mountain," Martin told Andy. "We'll leave you two girls together," he said, for the second time that weekend. More than ever Fiarette wished she could get rid of Marabea. If she had been all by herself, Martin would have asked her to come. She watched them drive off. "I wonder if he's too young to know what's going on in my mind when I look at him? I bet he thinks I'm real sweet. He has no idea."

Marabea was furious. "How can you talk that way when you have Martin?" Her voice was not as mad as she felt.

"I don't *have* anyone, Marabea. People don't *have* each other." She exaggerated the word as best she knew how and then said in a smart-ass voice, "Victory is a guy with a tattoo that says FOLLOW ME."

"You're misled."

"Mislead? Misled. I'm not misled at all — I just don't want to be a permanent fixture."

"What if somebody wants to be part of your life?"

"I don't encourage it."

"It must be nice not to need anybody."

"It's not that I don't need anybody. As a matter of fact," her voice sweetened up, "right now I need you."

"You do? For what?"

"Tonight I'm going to fix it so we all end up at the pond together. I know Martin will get tired first, he'll probably go up to bed about ten, and then I want you to promise me you'll leave next. As soon as possible." She half smiled, knowing she couldn't be clumsy; by no means did she have Marabea in the palm of her hands.

"I don't believe you're saying things like this to my face."

"Well, I didn't exactly invite you up here this weekend."

"You would never have invited me." For the first time Fiarette noticed how big her eyes were.

Slow down, she told herself. She would be smart; she would coax Marabea any way possible to get what she wanted. "Oh, I would have invited you, probably more than once. Only not on a holiday weekend, they're too hectic."

"I'm not having a hectic weekend," Marabea said.

"Promise me, Marabea, promise me — you'll get tired tonight, or you'll feel like watching television — that's even better," — her voice raced with fervor — "you don't have to go to sleep, you can watch a movie — there's cable here, we get AMC, I think this week is the Ray Milland festival — just leave me in the moonlight with that kid."

"You really love to be irresistible, don't you?"

Fiarette grinned.

At eight o'clock that evening they all ended up by the pond.

Every time someone walked by, the frogs leaped back in the water one by one.

"I won this at a penny social," Fiarette told Marabea, as she lit a thick yellow candle with silver glitter on it. At the other end of the pond she had placed candles on the flat arms of some Adirondack chairs. The two girls sat around a small metal table shaped like a flower petal; in the shadow of the candles was a 64-ounce blender of piña coladas.

"People are afraid of what they don't know," Marabea said. "They think they're so smart, but they don't know what's going to happen tomorrow. That makes us all pretty much equal."

"What are you talking about stuff like that for?" Fiarette asked. "Let's just cool out." Martin and Andy sat close enough so they could hear what was being said but far enough away where it was perfectly okay not to say a word.

"People are afraid of being found out. We know what we're no good at."

"Who wants to go in the water?" Fiarette leaped up and over towards Martin and Andy.

"Well, this is a first. You haven't been in that pond all summer."

"I told you I'd go in."

"It's not even that hot.

"Oh, sure it is," Fiarette said, gathering her dress up to her waist and dipping her toe in and then her foot until she was on the last stone slab. She lifted her dress over her head and turned to throw it to Andy, who, she was happy to see, was the closest one. "Here, catch," she said, and dove in the pond. She floated into the darkness and swam out of sight toward the other end where more candles flickered. The top of the water was warm but from her waist down it was cool. She liked the way the water cradled her. Her hair was wet now and felt longer than ever. She couldn't hear a thing. It didn't sound as though anyone was talking — she didn't think they would. What would the three of them have to talk to each other about? This was the way she liked it, floating and sitting on top of the world at the same time.

Martin was bored. Fiarette's ramshackle moods, he was beginning to think, were masterminded by her to secure something she was unable to ask for in a normal way. When other people were around, she had no trouble being illuminating and having a great time. But when it was just the two of them, she became almost forlorn. Martin got up from his chair, too tired to translate.

"Don't let me get in the way of a good time. You guys stay down here. I'm going back. Goodnight," he nodded to Marabea.

Marabea wished Andy would leave, too. Wouldn't it be wonderful if Fiarette could come out of the water and Andy would have disappeared and Marabea could tell her Andy decided he was too tired, too. She tried hard to will it.

"Where's Martin?" They saw Fiarette's head bob up out of the dark water at their feet.

"He went back."

"Throw me my dress, Marabea." She slipped it over her wet body and sat in the chair.

Marabea watched Andy looking at Fiarette's clinging dress and said to her, "Aren't you cold?"

"No," Fiarette said, pulling her knees up to her chest and clasping her hands around them. But you know what I'd love?" She smiled. "Some hot coffee. Would you mind, Marabea? I'm too wet to go in the house."

Reluctantly Marabea moved. Fiarette watched her disappear down the path. The time had come.

"So." Fiarette said, looking at Andy, leaning towards him, letting her shoulders delicately push her breasts together. He could see everything in the candlelight.

"So." Andy said, knowing he didn't sound as good as she did.

"You're so quiet people are going to think you have nothing to say." Andy was sure she would start to move closer.

"Are you and my uncle going to get married?"

"Oh, God, no." She moved off the chair and onto the grass almost at his feet. "I'm not ready to marry anyone. But he's a great man. If I was going to marry anyone, it would be him. He's just like me in the winter — he gets cold but he never thinks of putting on a hat." Andy didn't laugh. "Your uncle is really an extraordinary person. I think anyone who knows him grows because of it."

The sky lit up with firecrackers. It had been too cloudy the night of the Fourth but now it was clear, hot and dark.

"Look at them," Andy said, dazzled by the flickering sky.

I wonder if he's a firecracker in bed, she thought. She knew a lot of willful and irrational moves and if she had to she would use them all. She would not be satisfied until she had him.

They could hear footsteps coming towards the pond. Marabea turned a bend and stood there holding a tray with a coffee pot and three mugs.

"I mixed the milk in the coffee already. I hope everybody likes milk," she said seriously.

Fiarette got angry when she saw three mugs. She walked towards her and lifted the tray from her hands. She whispered. "Get lost, Marabea. I mean it. Get lost." She wanted to wring her neck. She took the coffee pot and two mugs and quickly handed back the tray with one mug on it. Marabea took it and walked away. It was hard to see what was in her eyes.

"What do we want with coffee when we have all this left?" She raised the blender high and poured from it filling Andy's glass to the top. "Isn't it a lot nicer sleeping in the country?"

"I think I was dreaming all night." he said. "One part was

real strange."

Fiarette hoped it had something to do with her. "What was it?"

"All I remember for sure is some words. Egg salad, kismet and the Bible. I don't know if someone said them to me or if they were written down or if they were graffiti on a wall or what. All I know is there was this feeling that each one counted; if you had all three, you would be happy. Each one had an important place."

"What do you think it meant, egg salad? Like a sandwich?"

"I guess so, but it was so clear in the dream. I guess it was a sandwich, on white bread, like when you're a kid and you take your lunch to school."

"And kismet?"

"Fate, I guess. Do you think kismet and fate are the same thing?"

"I'm not sure. I think fate is something that happens and kismet is a place you might bump into it."

"Through fate?" Andy smiled.

She smiled back, wanting an end to the talking, "and the Bible is the Bible."

"Yeah."

She poured just a few mouthfuls of piña colada for herself. She wanted to be sure Andy got most of it.

"You know," he said, "in the dream each thing was like a step towards something, or maybe they all happened together, I'm not really sure."

"You know you have a beautiful voice. When you start to speak, it sounds as though you're going to recite a poem."

"Thanks."

She could feel the buzz and wondered if she'd be able to walk.

"How old are you?" he asked.

"I don't know if I want to tell you."

"It doesn't matter," he said, feeling stupid.

"All right then, pick a number," she said brightly. She was still on the grass but closer than ever. They could feel each other's heat.

"Is that girl your friend?"

"Not exactly. She thinks hard times are like close links."

"She seems so mad at everything."

"It's her way of being worried." Fiarette's hair was wet and curly around her face.

"There's always something to be mad about," Andy said.

"You don't look like an angry young man to me," Fiarette said, standing up, wanting to be sure she could still get up on her feet. "I think I'll be going to Peru soon," she said.

"Really?"

"Really. I want to see Machu Picchu." She sat back down. "I want to see what it feels like to live in a lost city."

"It sounds awesome."

"I bet you'd find out all about egg salad, kismet and the Bible there. Maybe you ought to come with me." She looked into his face and wondered where he'd touch her first. She lingered with the thought, inspired by the thrill, and began to tinker with uncertain strategies.

It started raining. Out of nowhere. They watched the raindrops on the pond, saying nothing.

"Are you getting chilled?" she asked him, standing up again. "I feel great. I might even go for another swim."

He shivered.

"I saw that. You are cold. Do you want to go back?"

"No," he said. "Do you?"

"Nope." She poured the hot coffee into one of the mugs and, sipping with both hands, lowered herself onto the wet grass at his feet and sat facing him. She raised the coffee mug to his lips. He took a sip while she held it. The rain was coming down harder now and they were soaked. She placed the mug of coffee on the seat of his chair between his bare legs. He could feel it warm his thighs and his heart started to beat so fast he thought she could hear it. She pushed the mug of coffee closer and closer between his legs toward his body. She didn't want to give him a chance to say no. She was amazed and thrilled at her audacity. It was a story she never wanted to forget.

And he said, "Do you think people who really love each other ever feel like they don't?"

"Don't what?"

"Don't love each other."

"Oh, all the time," she said, lowering herself onto his chair. His face was right there and his kisses were shy, not insane like hers.

She was all legs. He looked at her thighs and couldn't believe she was his to touch. He thought about his Uncle Martin, how he must feel to have someone like this. He touched her breasts hard, then loosened his touch, softened it, wanting to know if his uncle did the same kind of things he was doing, wondering if she was going to compare the two of them. He wanted to ask, but he began to forget about it. He was so happy he felt like he was rocking.

And Fiarette was thinking: truth is inconvenient.

"Hi," the voice said, and she stood there, almost on top of them. "It's raining. I thought maybe you might not even notice — you were having such a good time."

"Are you fucking crazy?" Fiarette jumped up and tore over to her.

Marabea's voice was low and even, bright but measured. "I came down to get you. I was up in the bedroom alone watching you from the window. Thinking. Thinking what a special relationship we have. We understand each other without even trying. We're like two peas in a pod." She paused. "I see you finished all the liquor."

"There's something really wrong with you, Marabea." She turned away. "Come on, Andy, let's go back to the house."

Marabea put a hand on her arm. "You don't understand, Fiarette, I came to get *you*." And then, intimately, a hush over her words. "Say you're tired."

Andy sat there, not stirring, feeling he had nothing to do with it. Fiarette listened to this force gaining control. She could hear it clearly. Marabea sounded like she was in pain and Fiarette knew that whatever she said would be the wrong thing. It was too late for a moral resolution.

Fiarette started to walk away and felt something, first at her side, then moving to the center of her back. "What's in my back?"

"Does it hurt?"

"No. It doesn't hurt. Are you trying to hurt me?"

"I don't know what I'm trying to do." Marabea sounded believable. "Say you're tired. Say something. Just tell him you're tired. I mean it. And don't touch him while you're talking to him. Don't even look at him too long."

"Andy," Fiarette said finally, "I think I'm out of steam." She wanted to rub his neck and pull him to her. She wondered when she'd get another chance. "I'm going back to the house with Marabea and see what this is all about. See you in the morning. I think the night has come to an end."

"Don't get smart," Marabea said.

They started to walk away from the pond. The weeds and brush on either side of the narrow path were as tall as they were.

"Marabea, what's the matter?" Fiarette said in her nicest voice.

"I don't want you spending any more time alone with him tonight." Fiarette was shocked at the tone of her voice, like she was on a rampage.

"Are you interested in Andy?"

"No. I'm just interested in how many people are interested in you. And you're so nasty to all of them. You like to keep people in suspense."

Fiarette felt vaguely sorry for her. Marabea was like a sad song. But she was starting to get scared. She tried to think of it as not really happening to her. She was only shaping reaction, but reality was happening outside her. The incident was eerily familiar, a game she would have to work hard to win, but nothing to worry about. But Marabea's temper tantrum did not stop.

"Don't you feel even a little bit sorry for me?"

"Marabea, I can't do your suffering for you."

"The trouble with you is you have so much and you still want more."

"Wanting more just means people can't live in the present. I don't want more of anything."

"You have no sympathy."

"Why should I let your bad luck do damage to me? I don't even know you. You're the angry one. I'm not the angry one. I don't think that's having no sympathy."

"You know, it's not that you're that pretty; it's just that you're thin."

"What the hell is going on here?"

Marabea had a crazy smile on her face and started talking again. "You like to be in control, don't you?"

Fiarette wished she could be at the gym right now. She'd never miss another day. That morning she had heard some actress on TV talk about working out and how great it felt to push through the pain. Push through the pain.

"What do you think would happen if you weren't in control, if someone was in control of you?"

Fiarette said, "Why would anybody even want to be in control of me?" She understood now the deliberateness of the panic. Marabea had thought it all through. She could feel her toes curl. "I just like to be different."

"Everybody's different," said Marabea. "You just like to invent and reinvent yourself. That's what makes you different."

"I'm different and you're jealous, Marabea. That's what makes you so hard to get along with."

"And you, you're hard to get along with because that's what you enjoy. That makes it more of a sin." She thought things over for a minute and then, "You know I'm likely to do anything. Not an awful lot matters to me anymore. I don't get excited about too many things. But I'm not indifferent when it comes to you. I wish I had a stick of dynamite. I'd like to see buildings blow up in the sky and people floating. I'd like to see everything go up in smithereens. Do you know that word — smithereens? My mother used to say it a lot. I always knew exactly what it meant. It's the kind of word you can see."

"What's wrong with you, Marabea? I mean, really, what's wrong with you?"

"I never believed a thing you said."

"Like what?" She wanted to scream. She could not believe this was happening. She was going to be shot, murdered by this free-wheeling crazy person. By now she felt sure Marabea had a gun. She had felt it in her back and she thought she might even have seen it and she had no doubt it was real.

"You change your mind so fast, it's evil," Marabea told her. "You think people are toys. And you're an extravagant liar and you don't even know it. You don't give anyone a chance to just live in the middle. People like you think people like me are stupid and boring and there's more of us than there are of you. [What will Martin think when he finds me dead? Fiarette thought.] You don't have to pay a lot of attention to life to get things right. You don't know anything about worrying. You don't have to agonize."

"Who says I don't have to agonize?" Her voice was centered. "How do you know what goes on inside of me? How would you know how I feel about being lonely? Or about anything? Maybe I'm just as scared as you are."

Marabea was delirious with joy. This scatterbrained glamour, this raging dialogue was more than she had hoped for; it was the most attention Fiarette had ever paid to her.

"What is it you want?" Fiarette went on.

"I don't know yet. Let's go upstairs. To your bedroom. I want you to show me your bedroom," she said in a level voice.

"But you've already seen it."

"I want to see it again." Her voice was calm but definite; she wanted to see the bedroom again. Fiarette could not dispute the clarity.

Fiarette walked into the big bedroom with its bay windows that were almost floor to ceiling. She looked out the window at the pond in the distance. The candles were still burning.

"Look, Fiarette."

Fiarette turned around. She had never seen someone planted so firmly in a floor before. She had never seen a gun in someone's hands aimed in her direction. It wasn't aimed like it was ready to go off. But it was definitely aimed so it would be taken seriously.

Marabea was smug. "You're going to listen to everything I have to say. You're not going to slip away to sleep with one of your boyfriends."

"What are you talking about? You're crazy. You're nuts!"

She continued in a velvety voice. "I'm not crazy at all. I'm angry, but at least I don't try to impress people." She took a wide brimmed straw hat off the painted bureau and popped it on, red ribbons trailing down the back of her head. "I might want you to take nude pictures of me."

Fiarette wondered if it would be better to talk or to keep

quiet. She did not even wonder where Andy or Martin were because the world had suddenly become very small, stifled. All that was left was the applause. It was over.

"Open your closet. I want to try on your clothes."

"My clothes?" Fiarette stared at her.

"Your clothes, yes, your clothes. I want to try on your clothes." Marabea's mouth was set and there was a fresh hell in her eyes. She looked like she was ready to pull her hair out. She was holding a strand of it with her left hand while she held the gun with her right.

Fiarette knew better than to tell her they wouldn't fit.

She flung open a bureau drawer and took out a pair of drawstring cotton shorts. "I want to try on these shorts." She pulled open the waistband until they looked like a huge square. "These will fit me."

She held the gun with one hand while she coaxed the shorts up over her tight jeans. They ripped going over her legs. She tugged and finally gave up. "I don't feel like taking my jeans off just to try these on." She stepped out of them and kicked them under the bed. "What do you wear when you go to bed?"

Fiarette didn't answer her.

"What do you wear?"

Fiarette nodded toward a small drawer and Marabea opened it and took out a beautiful fitted long white silk gown. It looked like something Merle Oberon would wear. She pulled it over her head, the gun still in her hand, over her extra large T-shirt, and tugged it down over her breasts until it ripped in two places.

Fiarette shrieked. "That was my mother's. I'll kill you, you crazy bitch. I hate you; I want you to stop touching my things."

The door swung open and Martin walked in the room. "What the hell's going on in here?" Marabea dropped the gun.

"She's fucking nuts. Just get her out of here."

"I think we should call the police," Martin said. "She does have a gun."

"Take the gun away from her and get her out of here."

Andy peeked into the room. Marabea looked up at him and said, "If I'm not here, who's going to tell the story about you and Andy?"

"I'm going to kill you, Marabea, if you don't get in that fucking car and move."

Martin wanted to raise his voice but found he could say nothing. He looked into Fiarette's eyes until she turned away and sat in a chair. She started to cry because Martin looked like he was about to. She kept her eyes down and wished she could feel her fingers stroke the back of Martin's neck just one more time. But you could feel love freezing.

Martin found Fiarette the next morning crying at the kitchen table. For a change she had gotten up before him. He had seen and heard her tears before. He wanted to forget about half truths, impertinent and unproductive. Oh, how they slowed you down, pushing you into stiff-legged excursions on the thin ice of personal grief, forcing you to compete on an exceptional number of levels.

"There's nothing left to say about us," his face went sour, "we haven't got a chance."

"There's a bus at eleven. I want to go home." She knew this was it.

He drove her to the bus station and they didn't say a word. In her eyes was the pain of a scoundrel. Outside the bus station two teenage boys were singing "Boogie Woogie Bugle Boy", harmonizing. Martin tried to remember being their age but could not.

★ ★ ★

He did not wait with Fiarette for the eleven o'clock bus, just dropped her off, and continued driving west across the county. He understood how much he had loved her. The cracks snaked in and out along the broken white line of the highway past signs advertising 104 acres for eighty-five thousand dollars and outdoor furniture and entertainment tonight and reminded him that he knew nothing. Past green trees and broken branches and the end, the screeching end, of growth. He drove slowly and let cars pass him; he was in no hurry. He was skimming time, being hypnotized by it, and he liked it. Once he got back to the house, there would be chores and chaos and no time to daydream about contradictions in terms. Who was she, Fiarette? Even her name had excited him. It sounded like it could belong to only her. He heard the wind in his ears; there were suddenly fewer cars. A truck going in the other direction with the letters NEWF on it and nothing else. A Ford wagon passed him and nothing else. The road curved and he kept going. The gas with guts — that's what the sign said next to the old white ice machine with the words "crystal clear ice" written on it. Time was poison, inhospitable, abrupt in its willingness. He prayed without knowing what for. He thought of the words of Paul Bowles: "Life itself goes wrong." He longed to find a place, and to stay in that place, an architect with no boundaries. He would make it a place that was stronger than its characters.

As he got closer to the house, Martin wondered if Andy would be man enough to stick around. He found him sitting on the porch. Martin walked up the stairs, his temples pulsing. "I understand this kind of thing. I was expecting it to happen. I just wish it hadn't been you." He looked squarely at him and sat in the porch rocker. He stopped talking long enough to see if Andy had something to say, but he didn't. "You know, when your mother had just married your dad and I had just married your aunt, the four of us used to go apple picking. It makes me smile now just to think about it. Everyone would core and slice the apples and your aunt would make the apple pie. Whatever apples were left, she would make apple crisp. Those are the days I want to remember. I can't begin to tell you how good they were."

He got up, distressed because the good times were dust; there were only shreds of the evidence of marksmanship. He went upstairs to the room where he had been doing his writing all summer, too drunk to write and too drunk not to. A mug of cold coffee was next to the typewriter. He swallowed the final few mouthfuls. He looked at a few paragraphs he had written earlier and crumpled the paper. He was too drunk to get up to throw away his wastepaper so he stuffed the pages into the mug. When the mug gets full of paper, full of all the words that don't work, I'll take a break, he thought. It had become too easy to drink in the country and it had all started with the piña coladas. Fiarette knew how to make them just right: coconut rum, coco lopez, pineapple juice, chopped ice and a banana. "The banana makes them creamy," she said.

CHAPTER 24

In Shadyside, Ohio a nine-year-old girl gets
swept away by a 200 foot high wave, 30 feet wide,
traveled for seven miles and lived to tell about it.

TV announcer: Aren't you a lucky little girl!
How do you think it happened?
Girl: I don't know — I can only dog paddle.

Fiarette arrived back in the city on a humid afternoon where the sky was gray and hazy and she was hot and sweaty. She still could not get used to wearing shoes — that had been one of the best things about summer in the country, wearing as few clothes as possible and shoes practically never. Inside her apartment she turned the water on for coffee and immediately realized there was no gas. No smell of gas, no pilot light to be lit, no hiss. The next morning she called the super. The super's wife had just had their first child and he had started doing coke with the two blondes on the second floor. He didn't know why there was no gas in her apartment. No one did — she called two of her neighbors, one on her floor and one two floors down, but no one was having a problem. She called Con Edison emergency. The woman was nasty. "I'd like to make an appointment," Fiarette said. "This is emergency," the woman said, "We don't make appointments."

Con Ed came and found a blocked riser and told her the line had to be blown out. They left her with a green notice tag. AVISO. To the Occupants. A Los Occupantes. Gas supply has been shut off. Se ha cortada el suministro de gas. The man had told her please not to call again until the repairs had been completed. She wondered if her Con Ed bill would be less.

The only thing she missed about not having gas was not being able to make coffee. The next two days she ran back and forth to the Korean deli buying cups of coffee for fifty-five cents, sometimes two at a time. She looked out the window, sipping a cup now, and saw a squirrel scurrying along the rim of the roof of the brownstone across the street. He scooted up the brick chimney, peeked inside, and then continued along the perimeter. She wondered if he knew the difference between a chimney and a tree. She didn't know what to do with herself. All she knew were recycled temptations. It was like having a collection of fringe. She picked up the telephone, not sure who she would call, and the line was dead. She couldn't believe she had no gas and now she had no phone. She didn't care about the phone — she didn't expect any calls and she didn't really want any. But she hated when things broke down; it was chronic and it made her mad. She picked up the phone and listened again and heard nothing: it was dead, no dial tone, no sound at all. The dead phone felt menacing. She didn't know what to do. She ran her finger around the dusty earpiece. She had never had anything happen to a telephone before. She looked in the white pages. For telephone repairs, see page 5. Call 611. She went downstairs to the telephone two blocks up on the corner. The telephone lady was very nice but told her they were booked up for the next two days and if it was determined that the problem was "in the instrument itself" she would be charged for maintenance. She got the quarter back for the phone call to the phone company which was the only good thing to happen in the past twenty-four hours. She went and bought another cup of coffee, came upstairs and wondered where the squirrel had gone. She looked through her refund coupons: she kept them in a long white envelope tacked on a bulletin board near her telephone. Most of the coupons expired before she got to use them.

Save fifty cents when you buy any size powder or liquid

Cheer. Expires 5/31.

Save one dollar on Revlon No-Sweat anti-perspirant, any product except trial size - expires 6/30.

The Cheerios and the Folgers had no expiration date.

Another dollar coupon for Cheer had expired on May 31. Three coupons for Maxwell House coffee all had expired June 31.

The plumber finally showed up with an aqua T-shirt and a dangling cigarette and kept saying "Jesus Christ." Finally, he said "Do you have a small step ladder?" She unwedged the ladder which she stored in the kitchen between the refrigerator and the wall and the dust mop and the blue broom. The plumber pulled the ladder from her with one hand and propped it against the wall, climbed a few steps and began yanking away the molding on the paneling behind her stove. She said nothing. She wanted to ask him please to come back tomorrow because she wanted to be alone. "Jesus Christ," he said, and walked out the door down the stairs to the basement. While he was gone, Fiarette picked up the phone but still no sign of life. The plumber returned with a helper, very thin all in blue. "We have to take this wall down," he said. He pulled away the sheet of paneling. She could hear him mutter. She could hear large chunks of plaster falling inside the wall; she wondered where it was landing. "That's what they call New York City life," he laughed. She hated them both. The man in blue was dark-skinned. He stared at her and said nothing. She hated him more than the other one.

At three o'clock the plumbers left for the day and she couldn't see where anything had been done.

She took a walk and went into Wendy's. A girl took her order and wrote it on an order pad and then handed the slip back for her to give to the counterperson. The order-taker's name was

Renee and she wore a gold-colored badge that said Employee of the Month. Fiarette wondered what it took to be named Employee of the Month at a fast food restaurant.

The next morning she got up early to do her laundry. In the Chinese laundry the lady was listening to Elton John. Fiarette looked at the Wascomat Junior W74 operating instructions and wondered if it was all right to put the detergent and bleach in Compartment 2 for the wash cycle while the soak cycle was still in progress. Laundry bags were for sale. She wondered if she should get a new one. They came in two sizes. She would get the smaller one which looked about the same size as the yellow cotton one she had now that was coming apart. She didn't think she could carry the bigger one; by the time it got full, it would be too heavy. They were made out of a shiny material; she wondered how many colors they came in; only two colors were displayed on the wall. The black one had a piece of paper pinned to it that said $4.50 and the red one said $5.50. The dollar sign was written in pencil and the numbers were written in pen. Maybe she should just use a pillowcase.

When it was dry, she packed up the laundry and crossed the street. She saw moving men coming out of her building with a flowered love seat. A neighbor across the street told her they were moving furniture out because someone had died; Fiarette remembered him, a Japanese man with black shiny hair that swung at his knees. He had subscribed to *Woman's Wear Daily* and always left last week's copy in the hallway in case someone wanted it.

Early the next day she decided to sell seven hats she had collected at yard sales and flea markets in the country. One white straw looked like a wedding cake. A pale pink pillbox with a band of chiffon petals reminded her of the kind of hats her mother used to wear on Easter Sunday. A blue and white straw was full of ribbons. The girl at Chameleon was curled up on the wide ledge of a big window.

"What kind of hats?"

Fiarette showed her.

"What are you asking?"

This was the part Fiarette had rehearsed. She was supposed to say "I have seven hats and I'd like twenty dollars." Instead she said, "Ten dollars for all of them."

"Come back after seven when the boss is here."

She remembered how excited she had gotten when she discovered an old hatbox from Albany full of hats at Our Lady of the Lake garage sale. Martin would always happily give her the few dollars to buy any hats she came across; he told her he loved the way she looked in them, but she was always afraid they would blow off.

On the way home she saw some graffiti.

Life is grisly.

Life is gruesome.

Ask Sarah. They took her on the boat because she saw something she shouldn't.

It spooked her.

That afternoon she went to the gym. The sanitary napkin machine in the ladies' locker room had the right-hand corner smashed in. There was no way anyone could get Stayfree Maxi, Carefree panty shields or Playtex tampons. The story was that someone who lost a 10K run was so angry she did it. Fiarette enjoyed the image. It was the kind of rigorous passion Fiarette dreamed of and she seemed to have more of it when she was in the weight room. She started concentrating hard on range of motion, full range, outer range, middle range and inner range; fully stretched muscles was the goal. Leverage and stability represented power and became her ambition. She held a barbell to her chest for just one second, relaxing the muscles so the weight could drop with the least resistance. She liked to do fast dead lifts; one of the guys told her it was great if you ever intended to throw a hammer. The movement was fast, merciless. She knew where her elbows should be to stay away from excessive lean-back. She knew how to use her thighs. She could make bar bells motionless. She felt like she could do balancing acts. It was a serious subject, a consummate design. If she felt edgy when she walked into the weight room, she was soon grinning at a job well done and just for her. When the grit started to waver she dried up and went home.

On the way home she stopped in Red Apple and, with a couple of yogurts and some fruit in her cart, got on the express line, ten items or less. The man in front of her was very heavy and his shirt hung out of his pants; he had six items in his cart. While the line slowly moved towards checkout, he left his cart in place and rushed off to get tins of smoked oysters and other kinds of canned fish until the six items grew to fourteen. Fiarette counted. Then he put in an Entenmann cake labeled the "classic" layer cake. It cost $6.79. Fifteen items. He then paid for as much as he could with food stamps. It was the first time Fiarette had ever seen anyone pay for food with food stamps.

The mood of the day had been sunny but suddenly it all changed. Head to head with too much quiet time. She wanted to hear herself talk. She wanted to hear her own voice. She was ready to talk to anyone. She picked a pretty woman with a T-shirt that said I Love The Underground Life.

"I love your shirt. Did you get it around here?"

They had stopped at a light going downtown on Seventh Avenue.

"It's a Tom Tom Club," she said. It sounded like Tum Tum. The name of Jesus was chalked on the corner croissant shop.

The last page in the *Sunday Times* book review had an item headed Heaven Hangs On. It said that in a recent Gallup poll, 71 per cent of the American public answered yes when asked whether they thought there was a heaven where people who have led good lives are eternally rewarded. Could there be a God and no heaven? Suddenly Fiarette understood what she had done. Until now it had been distilled recognition. Now she defined it as a sin; it was a sin because someone got hurt.

Martin tried to write. One day the following string of words came up.

> Moments on the moon,
> minor authorities
> da da da da da
> too soon, too soon.

He felt comforted by who he was. He smiled because more than ever he understood the temporariness of it all. The war was over but all the troops were not home.

When Marabea got home, her roommate told her to stay put because a note in the lobby said that the repairman wanted to get into as many apartments as possible because something was wrong with the building intercom. "You can talk and you can hear but you can't buzz anyone in." It would take a couple of days to figure out that the trouble was with the lock and not with the intercom after all.

Willy Saunders was in his early forties and wore a black cap that said HARDWARE. When he worked, he drove a truck. It was red and white and it was all he wanted to do. Until one day he got a job at the intercom company. He couldn't believe his good luck when he saw Marabea's name on the buzzer.

"Intercom repair," he said cheerily outside her apartment door.

She opened the door and recognized him instantly. "I was hoping you'd be home," he said, smiling. "Old buddy." He hugged her.

"You're not mad at what happened?" She opened the door wider.

"Nah. Me? Hold a grudge? Nah. Besides, I guess I liked you enough to forgive you." He wore clean dungarees with the pleat steamed in. She smiled and let him in.

As soon as he was inside the door and feeling comfortable, his voice changed.

"You know, good ideas don't come easy and I wasted that one on you." His teeth were all over his lips.

"You could have done it with somebody else."

"I could have killed you when that bag broke at my feet. What were you trying to do, get me caught? You walked out of there like you never saw me in your life."

She said nothing.

"The more I look at you, the madder I get." His fingertips grazed her cheeks. Then they snapped. Frivolously. Then harder.

"Stop," she said, "you're starting to hurt me." Her voice staggered, a child who did not understand.

The first blow was so violent that it broke the bone of her eye.

Minutes later Willy Saunders was at the foot of the 59th Street Bridge throwing the biggest rocks he could find at passing cars. It was obvious he would get picked up and that was what he wanted. He had just beat someone up, maybe to death; he would be safe in Bellevue or in jail. He would give his name as

Jimmy and they would give him the "Doe".

As usual, the girls all met for brunch on 72nd and Broadway that Saturday. One girl arrived breathless and told a group of single women that she had woken up to find her roommate dead. In the bathtub.

"Suicide?"

"I don't know."

"Well, what did you do?"

"Nothing."

"You didn't call the police?"

"No."

"Did you empty the water?"

"No."

"You'd better go home. The police always want to talk to the one who found the body,"

There was no sign of forced entry, a paragraph in the paper would say. Nothing was stolen. The first thing found in the apartment was a fortune from a cookie that said "Keep this fortune; it'll bring your heart's desires." The next day someone in the building got nervous and posted a notice in the hallway to be extra careful who you let into the building. From that day forward her roommate lived in terror.

Fiarette didn't see the write-up in the paper; after a few weeks she never thought about Marabea again. She was just glad she never saw her in Bagel Buffet any more, which is where she was now.

"That's where you get your weight from," the grandmother said to the chubby ten year old across from her. But he kept right on eating his fried onion rings. Fiarette noticed that in addition to a dozen varieties of bagels and bagel chips, Bagel Buffet was now offering bagelettes. A woman behind her was going deaf and talking loud, "I was in charge of a business that sold a million and a half dollars worth of merchandise a day." She had struck up a conversation with a young girl sitting at her booth and asked if she spoke Spanish.

When Fiarette left, she strolled down side streets which were cooler, past places with names like Solo Air Conditioning and Blue Sky Electric. A bus had trouble turning a corner and a taxi cab squeaked. The park now had a quiet zone. She thought of Martin and how she was able to disguise herself.

In the city you sweep the leaves and in the country you rake them.